The *Excalibur* began
Sammy activated the graviton drive. They would be in
position to jump in a minute. Suddenly Eric's suspicion
that Strem was hiding a crucial fact became a certainty.

"How long?" Strem asked. He looked scared and
jubilant. Eric didn't know which worried him more.

"Fifteen seconds." Sammy said. "Fourteen . . . Twelve
. . . Ten . . ."

"We're not going to Tau Ceti, are we?" Eric demanded. Strem did not answer. Eric grabbed him by
the collar and yanked him around. "*Are we?*"

"Eight . . . Seven . . . Six . . ."

"*Where are we going?*" Eric shouted.

Too late. It was done. Eric had the sensation of
stepping outside himself. When the blink of time and
space was complete, Eric repeated his question, with
one word changed.

"*Where are we?*"

"Outside," said Strem. "Beyond the Tachyon Web. . . ."

Bantam Books of Related Interest
Ask your bookseller for the titles you have missed

A WIZARD OF EARTHSEA by Ursula LeGuin
THE TOMBS OF ATUAN by Ursula LeGuin
THE FARTHEST SHORE by Ursula LeGuin
VERY FAR AWAY FROM ANYWHERE ELSE
  by Ursula LeGuin
EXILES OF COLSEC by Douglas Hill
THE CAVES OF KLYDOR by Douglas Hill
INTERSTELLAR PIG by William Sleator
SINGULARITY by William Sleator
DEVIL ON MY BACK by Monica Hughes
THE FALLEN COUNTRY by Somtow Sucharitkul
DRAGONSONG by Anne McCaffrey
DRAGONSINGER by Anne McCaffrey
DRAGONDRUMS by Anne McCaffrey
OUT OF SIGHT, OUT OF MIND by Chester Aaron
KITEMAN by Alfred Reynolds

THE TACHYON WEB

Christopher Pike

BANTAM BOOKS
TORONTO · NEW YORK · LONDON · SYDNEY · AUCKLAND

RL 7, IL age 11 and up

THE TACHYON WEB

A Bantam Spectra Book / November 1986

All rights reserved.
Copyright © 1986 by Christopher Pike.
Cover art copyright © 1986 by Kevin Johnson.
This book may not be reproduced in whole or in part, by
mimeograph or any other means, without permission.
For information address: Bantam Books, Inc.

ISBN 0-553-26102-9

Published simultaneously in the United States and Canada

Bantam Books are published by Bantam Books, Inc. Its trademark,
consisting of the words "Bantam Books" and the portrayal of a
rooster, is Registered in U.S. Patent and Trademark Office and in
other countries. Marca Registrada. Bantam Books, Inc., 666 Fifth
Avenue, New York, New York 10103.

PRINTED IN THE UNITED STATES OF AMERICA

KR   0 9 8 7 6 5 4 3 2 1

To Lisa

1

Eric Tirel first learned of the plans for the illegal space jump from his best friend only a week before it actually took place. Had Eric had longer to think about the immensity of what they were attempting, he might have backed out. Had his best friend told him half of what was planned for the trip, Eric probably would have turned him over to the authorities and asked for a reward. As it was, Eric found out the truth much too late to make any difference.

Eric Tirel's best friend was Strem Hark, and besides being an established fun-loving con man, Strem was always late. Eric had been waiting over an hour at the window of the observation tower in the center of Baja Spaceport for Strem to show up. Yet the delay had not bothered him. The view from the top of the tower was fine company: long silver starships rising slowly—practically soundlessly—over the flat blue ocean atop the thrust of their graviton drives, glistening in the orange evening sun like gigantic fireflies.

He often caught the bullet monorail down from Los

Angeles to the spaceport simply to watch the ships disappear over the hazy edge of the Earth's atmosphere. He had been to the moon and the planets more times than he could remember and had even once made a hyper jump to and from the Vega System, but it was as though he were a kid from the end of the twentieth century.

Spaceships always seemed somehow novel and magical to him. It had been his intention to join The Patrol and spend the rest of his life in space. That is, until the academy had returned his entrance application with a form letter that said they didn't want him, without even saying why. Just thanks but no thanks, and with High Commander General Griffin's *personal* signature *stamped* on the bottom. Well, it was their loss. He probably couldn't have spent the rest of his life taking orders from those jerks, anyway. It was bad enough listening to his parents reminding him to study more.

"I've figured out what we're going to do over spring break," Strem said to his back, finally arriving.

Eric did not immediately turn around. One of The Patrol's cruisers—easy to identify with their distinctive orange and black stripes—was approaching from the southwest. It was possible this very cruiser had hours ago been exploring outside The Tachyon Web, the network of ninety thousand hyper-spatially connected satellites The Patrol had strung around their corner of the galaxy to prevent civilian pilots from making hyper jumps beyond the confines of The Union. Eric appreciated The Patrol's desire not to have human beings hopping all over The Milky Way, but he often wondered what they might be hiding out there. Of course, there was the persistent rumor that the human race was engaged in a bloody interstellar war with a hideous alien race that the authorities were afraid to admit for fear of causing a widespread panic. He was not too keen on the war theory. He had come to the conclusion that the government only wanted to keep track of all the civilian pilots for tax purposes. But, since The Patrol had rejected him, he probably would never know for sure.

"Do I have any say in this?" Eric asked, not really offended at Strem's assumptive planning. Strem always had a wild scheme going. Eric had decided a long time ago it was his purpose in life to keep Strem from accidentally killing himself.

"Absolutely not."

"In that case, *what* are we doing?" he asked, turning around and wondering at his friend's exceptionally broad grin. A good percentage of the girls at school were in love with Strem. Eric probably would have been jealous—actually, it did bother him occasionally—if Strem hadn't so fully deserved their affection. Besides having the best physique strenuous exercise could build, and a face that was both humorous and strong, topped with uncombable blond hair and lit with wild blue eyes, Strem was always upbeat. It was in the record book that once when a lunar shuttle had lost its directional beam and was threatening to crash into the harsh moonscape, a passenger aboard had casually remarked that at least they would have a crater named after them. Then again, Strem had been his only witness when insisting that it had been himself who had made the famous comment.

"We're going on a little trip," he said, leaning with his back to the window. The observation corridor was dim, having only the late sun for light, and practically deserted. "How does Easter in the Tau Ceti System sound?"

"Your uncle?" Eric said automatically, feeling his pulse quicken. Strem's uncle was a trader and had one of the

next-to-impossible-to-get pilot licenses. He also owned
an aging twenty-second-century freighter named *Excalibur* whose graviton drive still packed enough horsepower to push the ship far enough away from the sun to
launch a respectable hyper jump. Strem's uncle had
never before offered to take them anywhere. Eric would
kiss the old goat's feet if he'd had a change of heart
about passengers. When Eric had traveled to the Vega
System it had exhausted a year's savings in a weekend.
But it had been worth it. A freebie was almost too
much to hope for. Especially to Tau Ceti. There was a
moon there circling the tenth planet that was one gigantic diamond.

Strem nodded. "Uncle Dan just signed a contract
with a distributor on Ceti Six for several thousand fiberoptic wardrobes. You know those new clothes that light
up whenever you move or get excited?"

"I wouldn't be caught dead wearing one of those
outfits," Eric muttered, not really caring what the cargo
was. "What made him change his mind about taking on
useless baggage such as ourselves?"

"It's a long story."

Eric had heard *that* line before. What Strem was
really saying was, *"You don't want to know."*

"How long will we be there?"

Strem shrugged. "For as long as we like."

"Your uncle is scarcely in one place two days in a
row. How can it be for as long as we like?"

"Because he's not coming," Strem said matter-offactly. Then he burst out laughing. Familiar with his
style—Strem loved theatrics when revealing a secret—
Eric let him finish.

"He's being sued," Strem said finally, chuckling. "A
mining company on Titan is accusing him of failing to
deliver much-needed equipment after being paid in

advance. Can you imagine? He's to be in court from now until next month."

"*Did* he deliver the equipment?"

Strem waved away the question. "He tried. What else can a man do? Besides, it was the mining company's fault that they didn't get the stuff."

"How so?"

"They should have known better than to pay him in advance."

Eric shook his head. "I don't understand. We can't take *Excalibur* to Tau Ceti."

"Yes, we can!" Strem said, his hands becoming animated. "I can pilot the freighter, especially with Sammy's help. There'll be no problem."

Sammy Balan was a good friend and the younger brother of the well-known Lien Balan, who was responsible for many of the sophisticated capabilities of the navigational computers in the most-advanced space cruisers. As far as computers were concerned, Sammy was perhaps as gifted as his brother. If left alone, Sammy could probably get them to Tau Ceti. Nevertheless, Eric was beginning to have his doubts.

"This isn't going to work. We can't—"

"The distributor needs the goods next week," Strem interrupted. "If he doesn't have them by then, the deal's off." He put a hand on Eric's shoulder. "Don't worry."

"Aren't you overlooking a few minor details? How can we get past customs and out of the solar system? They'll want to talk to your uncle, and if he's not aboard, they won't give us clearance."

Strem stashed away his merry manner and glanced around to be sure no one was listening. Their nearest company was a passionately kissing young couple and they obviously had other things on their minds. "Sammy has been working on tying a holographic film in with *Excalibur*'s computer," Strem said quietly.

"And the film is of your uncle," Eric muttered, catching on fast. Strem was implying that they were going to try to make Central Control believe Uncle Dan was aboard when he wasn't. With the quality of present-day recording equipment, a holograph was practically undetectable from the original, especially when transmitted to a point far away, as it would be in this case. The visual technicalities of the plan did not trouble him. It was the programming of the image's responses to Central Control's variable questions during the customs procedure that would be dangerous. Others had tried it in the past and they were now working in chemical factories on Mercury. "Is Sammy's older brother helping with the programming?" he asked.

Strem shook his head. "This is just between us, believe me."

Whenever Strem said, *"Believe me,"* it was always a bad sign. "This is illogical. If your uncle is in court and is also supposed to be on his ship going to Tau Ceti, someone somewhere will put two and two together and blow the whistle."

"He'll be in court in person. Who's going to check to see if he's elsewhere? Central Control will have no reason to check with the judicial system."

That made sense, sort of. "I'm surprised your uncle is taking such a risk, having us deliver this shipment. If we get caught, he could lose his pilot license." And what would happen to *them*, Eric wondered, if Central Control hauled them in? He had never been particularly fond of Mercury. Air-conditioning or not, it was always hot there.

"From the hints he's dropped, the miners on Titan are going to make sure he loses it, anyway. This shipment is worth a small fortune. He may as well get in one last big score while he can."

Strem always had an answer for everything. "What's our percentage?"

"That's still being negotiated. Come on, what do you say?"

Eric had another dozen objections to raise, but none came out. What he was going to do over spring break had been weighing on his mind. He hadn't been looking forward to a couple of weeks of watching movies and hanging out at the beach by himself. Strem had previously mentioned that he would be spending the vacation with his latest girl, Jeanie Clayway, and Sammy had also indicated he would be busy with his girlfriend, Cleo Rettson. If the exotic scheme came off, Eric figured the two girls would also be coming to Tau Ceti.

He hoped he wouldn't appear the odd guy out. He didn't have a girlfriend at the moment. Actually, he had never had one, though he dated fairly regularly. He liked to think he hadn't found anyone that measured up to his standards but in reality he would have been very happy to have had a relationship with either of the last two girls he'd taken out. Unfortunately, neither Carol nor Barb were returning his calls. He wasn't sure why. Both of them had appeared to enjoy his company. He suspected that he just didn't do it for them, physically that was. He wasn't every female's fantasy but he knew he wasn't ugly. He wasn't as tall or as strong as Strem, but regular running had given him a firm wiry frame, and he saw a lot of the sun and had an excellent tan. His features were dark, his black hair long and curly. Others often remarked upon how thoughtful he appeared, even deep, and he did, in fact, excel in school. The potential was obviously there. Carol and Barb just didn't know what they were missing. A shame *he* knew what *he* was missing; they had both been gorgeous.

What the hell, The Patrol didn't want him and neither did the girls. He needed a change of scenery. "Okay," he said.

Strem did a double take. "What do you mean?"

"I'll go with you. It sounds like fun."

Apparently Strem had expected to have to spend more time convincing him. "You're not worried that we'll get arrested?"

"I'm worried that we'll get killed. Why should I worry about getting arrested?"

Strem slapped him on the shoulder. "I can see I've been a good influence on you, after all." He glanced at the necking couple. It reminded him of something. "I guess you've figured that we're taking Jeanie and Cleo?"

"Fine with me, as long as Cleo doesn't bring her snake." Sammy's girlfriend had a ten-foot-long python. Sometimes it seemed she liked her snake more than Sammy, which didn't bother Sammy one bit. He was obviously more attached to his computers. The two had an interesting relationship. "Do their parents know?"

"Are you kidding? *All* our parents are going to think we're safely on Mars. Record a couple of videos and give them to Clark. He's heading out that way next week. He'll send them over the ordinary channels to our parents."

Eric nodded. Tachyon or instantaneous transmission between Earth and Mars was expensive. Their parents would expect them to use standard electromagnetic broadcasts, and traveling at only the speed of light, such an old-fashioned medium would disallow two-way communication. Their parents need never know. Eric was not crazy about lying to them but neither was he going to lose any sleep over it.

"It would be great," Strem added, "if you could bring a girl, too."

Eric looked out the window. The Patrol cruiser had landed and the crew was being shuttled off the wide concrete field. "You know I don't have a steady girlfriend. How can I talk someone into spending a week with me in a cramped spaceship that stands a good chance of being blown out of the sky?"

"Appeal to the adventurous side in her!"

"In *who?*"

"Get any girl at school. There's lots of them. How about Carol or Barb?"

"They haven't called me in a couple of weeks."

"Call them."

"I have. More times than I can remember."

Strem was not insensitive. He quickly changed his approach. "You're right. They're more trouble than they're worth. If I had my way, just us three guys would go."

"What's stopping you from having your way?"

"Hey, don't try to analyze me when I'm acting the nice guy." He peered out the window, not at the ships and the conveyors laden with cargo and the scurrying uniformed workers, but at the swollen red sun, barely scraping the burning horizon. And his entire manner changed. One instant he was smiling, then suddenly he seemed worried. More than the vagueness of a couple of his answers, this brief falter made Eric suspect he was not telling the whole truth about the illegal trip. "It's not very bright," Strem said softly.

"What do you mean?"

"Compared to a blue star, for example. Or a nova." He glanced at Eric out the corner of his eye. "Do you know much about novas, Eric?"

Strem seldom addressed him by his name. "I know

they give off a tremendous amount of energy." He paused. "Why do you ask?"

Strem took his time answering, as though he were debating whether to answer at all. "I hear there is a nova in the Andromeda Sector."

"How close?" Every year there were several novas in the galaxy, but since the development of interstellar travel, there had not been one in the Earth's vicinity. It would make an interesting study for the astronomers.

"Close enough."

"Where did you hear this?"

"Does it matter? My sources are reliable. Take my word for it."

"Why did you bring it up just now?"

"Don't you find the information interesting?"

"Certainly. But . . . ?"

"That's why I told you. I knew you would be interested." Strem looked again at the setting sun, the sharp edge of the ocean cutting it in half, to a quarter, an eighth, before swallowing it all together. "Perfect," he whispered, nodding to himself as artificial light warmed up overhead.

"Have you suddenly become sentimental about sunsets, or what?" Eric asked.

Strem shook himself, as he would from a nap, and stepped away from the window, grabbing the top of Eric's arm and half pulling him down the corridor toward the elevators. The passionate couple had left and for a moment they were alone. Strem's mood, or whatever it had been, had passed. "Do you still want to rent a minisub and see if we can ram some sharks?"

That was why they had originally decided to meet in Baja. "Sure. But you didn't answer my question."

Strem laughed. "The only thing I feel sentimental about right now is the five-percent commission I'm trying to squeeze out of my uncle for delivering the cargo."

Eric figured he could question him further at another time. "You'll be lucky if you get one percent."

"I'd take it," Strem agreed, hurrying him along at his usual frantic pace. "Hey, I just thought of someone you can ask on this trip. Dentenia Soulete—she'd be perfect. She's not that bright, but she knows how to answer the phone and say yes. Here's what you'll do . . ."

Strem proceeded to bless him with a dozen lines that were guaranteed to stimulate Dentenia's lust for danger, space travel, and witty young men. Eric only half listened. He hardly knew Dentenia—though she had a superb body and he wouldn't have minded knowing her intimately—and couldn't imagine calling her. He was thinking of novas, exploding stars that saturated space with incalculable torrents of energy. The Andromeda Sector was not in the direction of Tau Ceti and Strem's commission. It was a shame in a way that they wouldn't have time to swing over for a quick peek. Of course that was for the best. God only knew what the emissions from a nearby nova could do to their equipment.

2

The dawn was sudden and dazzling as they ploughed out of the Earth's shadow into the glare of the sun five hundred miles above the cloudless Sahara. Eric immediately snapped down his visor, but not before he began to see stars that weren't there.

They were in a ferry halfway between Space Station One and *Excalibur*, floating away from the massive pinwheel that oversaw all travel within the solar system to the freighter that housed Strem and his girlfriend. The ferry was homed onto a directional beacon aboard *Excalibur* and would arrive at the freighter's bay doors without human assistance. Nevertheless, Sammy Balan was keeping a close eye on their approach, which was reassuring to Eric.

Sammy was as cautious as he was intelligent. Because he was so quiet, kids at school often mistook him as cold, and it was true his mind seemed to more closely parallel the working of a machine than a person.

Sammy's attention to detail, however, did not apply to his personal appearance. When he dressed in the morning, it was as though he put on the first thing his hand touched and didn't always check to see if it was a viable piece of clothing. Pale and underweight, his short stature was not helped by a chronic slouch. His one physical virtue was his long wavy brown hair, which managed to maintain a lustrous sheen despite infrequent washings. Yet he had mentioned cutting it all off. Sammy didn't care what he looked like.

"What do you think the chances are that we will get away with this?" Eric asked. They were sitting before rows of colored buttons and a single dark blue screen traced with shifting speed and distance graphs. A wide window curling back from the tip of the hull provided them with the breathtaking view of the Middle East. Because the ferry was used only for short trips, it was powered by simple chemical rockets and had no artificial gravity. If he were to unfasten his seat belt, he would float away. But he had recently eaten and wasn't in the mood for acrobatics.

"There are many variables," Sammy said. "It's hard to know."

"A ball park estimate would be fine."

"I'd give us a two out of three chance of being allowed to make a hyper jump."

"I was hoping you would have said a ninety percent chance."

"I may in fact be overly pessimistic. It all depends what Central Control asks our holograph of Strem's uncle. It was impossible for me to program it to respond to every variation."

"Will Strem be helping you pilot *Excalibur*?" he asked, trying to keep the tension out of his voice. He hadn't slept much last night and when he had, he'd had nightmares of calling his parents and telling them he wouldn't be home for dinner for about five years.

"Let's hope not," Sammy said flatly.

The growing *Excalibur* began to blot out the African continent. There was a brief nudge as the ferry braked. Perhaps when the freighter had been constructed it had been worthy of being named after the mythical sword, but six decades later, moored in orbit beside numerous modern craft, it looked like a clunker. A bulky gray cylinder, its living quarters and control deck were squeezed into a spherical compartment that was stuck like a Ping-Pong ball at one end. It would undoubtedly be retired soon. And yet, compared to the interplanetary ships of a couple of centuries ago, it was incredibly fast. The rear section was devoted to the cargo bay and the graviton drive, and the latter could propel them out of the solar system at about a third the speed of light, to a point sufficiently distant from the sun and planets to where they wouldn't snap in two initiating a hyper jump.

The hyper drive itself took up as much space as an ordinary desk. Out of their group, only Sammy had more than an inkling of the mechanics of the Unified Field that made it work. Once he had tried to explain the intricacies to Strem and Eric, and they had both ended up with headaches.

"Is Cleo aboard?" Eric asked.

Sammy half smiled, rubbing his eyes, which were red and tired. He must have been working overtime this last week to outwit Central Control's final check. That would not come until they were outside the orbit of Neptune, where a smaller version of The Tachyon Web had been erected to momentarily halt all traffic. A hundred years ago, when pilot licenses had first been issued, one had to pass through a strict customs aboard Space Station One just to leave Earth orbit. Now only those making hyper jumps were closely watched and even that scrutiny was done from a distance—Central Control had complete confidence in their methodology. Eric could feel the sweat gathering between his skin and his green flight suit. It was going to be a long day.

"She's on Mars, visiting an aunt," Sammy answered. "We'll pick her up before we head out."

"Is she bringing her snake?"

"Probably."

"I can hardly wait. Is Strem's uncle aboard?" Eric was not sure he wanted to meet the man again. After talking to Uncle Dan he always felt as though he should check to make sure he still had his wallet.

"He filled out the necessary paperwork, hopped over to *Excalibur* to make it look proper, and immediately snuck back to the station. He's probably back on Earth by now."

Approximately a hundred yards from docking, *Excalibur* eclipsed the sun. Eric peered outside, away from Earth, eagerly awaiting the stargazing he could do once they got out into space. He felt the jolt of the ferry's rockets fine-tuning their rendezvous. After dropping the people off, the ferry would retrace its steps alone back to Station One.

As the gray walls began to envelop them, he felt the artificial gravity generated by a component of the graviton drive press him into his seat. A couple of scrapes and bumps followed under his feet as they came to a complete stop on slip-fitting tracks. The door slid shut at their back and atmosphere poured into the air lock with an intense but brief roar. A flashing red light on the control board turned a solid green. There was a loud hiss as the ferry's seals peeked open. Eric felt a sudden rush of fear and almost asked to be taken back. What kept him going was nothing heroic. He simply thought of how lonely and bored he would be over spring break, and quickly climbed out.

They found Strem and Jeanie on the control deck. Their hellos were brief. With the tension in the room, they could have been going into battle.

A three-dimensional holographic cube dominated the center of the bridge, projecting schematics of their course in relationship to the planets, the latter's gravitational fields wavering in the haunting red background glow as though they were living ghosts. Taking a seat at the navigational computer, Sammy performed a quick systems check. As he did so, the transparent holographic cube sparked with unwinding white threads representing possible courses for *Excalibur* on its way out of the solar system. Eric noted how each line curved around a bright red dot—Mars and Cleo.

"We have clearance," Strem said, coming up behind Sammy, glancing out the windows, which were uncovered, turned toward the cloud-shrouded Asian continent. "Let's get out of here."

"One minute," Sammy said. "The ferry is still clearing. Did your uncle get the seal on the Preeze Cap repaired? The board shows minor pressure discrepancies." The Preeze Cap was a sophisticated circulation pump that helped keep the graviton drive from overheating. It used old-fashioned ethylene glycol.

"Yes," Strem said. "Do you need help plotting our course?"

"Absolutely not, thank you."

"Are you as scared as me?" Jeanie asked Eric, leaning beside him against the unlit panel that held the settings for the hyper drive. She was dressed in a black leotard, and her bushy brunette hair was tied with a yellow ribbon in a ponytail that reached to her waist. Sweat glistened on her bare arms from dancing to burn off her nervousness before they had arrived.

Jeanie was one of their school's cheerleaders and, after graduating, planned to study ballet, which she would certainly excel at—she looked graceful simply walking across campus. An uncomplicated person to the extent of being slightly dull, she compensated for any personality deficiencies with a fresh beauty that occasionally made Eric wonder if he wouldn't chase after her if say, Strem were to meet with a sudden and unexpected accident.

Eric thought of Dentenia; she had similar seductive legs, and Strem had been right that she knew enough to answer the phone. But he had been wrong about her automatic yes. She had given him a brisk no just before hanging up. He was still wondering why he had called her—at least when Carol and Barb didn't want to see him, they were polite enough to say they had to wash their hair or something.

"I've done worse things," Eric answered with a straight face.

"When?" Jeanie asked.

"In another life." He nodded towards Strem. "How did he talk us into this?"

"The same way as always—he kept on us until we said yes." She squeezed his hand. "Isn't it exciting?"

"Ask me after we get back home."

"We can go," Sammy pronounced. He glanced up at Strem, who nodded decisively. Sammy's right hand moved and as it did, so did the ship, India slipping from the windows and being replaced with starry space as *Excalibur* turned its back and main drive on the world below. The lights dimmed and the white streak within the holograph turned orange. A low deep hum filled the room, swiftly shifting into a high-pitched whine before suddenly cutting off into a ringing silence. Strem laughed and Jeanie gasped and Eric smiled as the Earth began to shrink like a colorful ball thrown into a deep dark well. In minutes they would be at full speed and in less than half an hour they would be entering Martian orbit. What a great way to start a vacation.

The time passed swiftly. Strem punched up a hamburger from the automatic galley and just about had to forgo chewing to finish it before the red star swelled into a sandstorm-torn world. Mars was in a foul mood and Eric was glad their destination lay elsewhere. The northern polar cap was practically obscured by airborne dust. Had they landed they would have had to stay inside the domed cities and been unable to go exploring, which would have been worse than laying on the beach at home.

"This is *Excalibur*," Sammy said into the mike. "Number FRE-4316-DH, requesting permission for F-level orbit slot."

A sweet feminine computer answered promptly. "Permission granted. Welcome to Mars, *Excalibur*. Please proceed to F-192, coordinates ten point two and six point seven. This is a passenger loading zone only. If you wish to remain in orbit longer than four hours you must request a new slot in a lower zone. Please respond that you have copied and understood."

"Gotcha, baby," Strem said over Sammy's shoulder.

"Response insufficient," the computer said. "We await copy and clarification."

"I wish I had a voice like that," Jeanie said with a sigh. While Strem had been swallowing his hamburger, Jeanie had gone to the cargo bay and fitted herself with a pair of Uncle Dan's fiber-optic pants, commonly called *opants*. When hanging in a closet, opants resembled bland gray leather pants or jackets. But once on a person, they glowed a spectrum of colors, depicting one's mood, which they determined by stealthily placed sensors in the wrists and armpits that were able to monitor the wearer's heartbeat, skin resistance, temperature, and arterial dilation. As Jeanie sighed, her arms shone a faint red, indicating desire. Eric feared if he pulled on a pair and hung around Jeanie, he'd look like a strawberry.

"I met the woman they got to record those tapes," Strem said. "She was a dog."

"*Excalibur* proceeding to F-192, coordinates ten point two and six point seven," Sammy said into the mike. "We shall occupy the position approximately one hour." He added, "Don't mind what my partner said about you."

"Copy and clarification complete. Reference to dog discarded."

Strem scratched his head. "I do remember her having a sense of humor." He paused. "So is Cleo in the F-zone?"

"Yes," Sammy said, typing in the coordinates. The cubical holograph now contained an exquisite two-feet-in-diameter simulation of Mars, surrounded by ten concentric nebulous shells, which Eric assumed were the zone levels. Sammy manipulated the controls and the real Mars outside the windows grew three times in size as a smaller version of Space Station One appeared off their port side, ringed with a myriad of glittering spacecraft. Glancing into a sensor plate, Sammy added, "Cleo's ferry is waiting. She must already be aboard it." He sent her a beacon to lock onto, and a voice that could have belonged to a six-year-old if it hadn't somehow managed to sound so tough came over the control deck's main speakers.

"Is that you, honey?"

"Which honey are you referring to, sugar?" Strem interrupted Sammy.

Cleo's laugh was high and loud. She had a powerful singing voice, which she exercised regularly in a band called The Meek Pulverizers—a revival of a very old style of music Sammy had once referred to as punk rock.

Eric never felt completely at ease around Cleo. She was wild. Her hair was seldom the same color two days in a row, and she was fond of chains and strange designs on her tight-fitting clothes. Without makeup and paraphernalia, though, she was a doll: short and dainty with fine red hair and an innocent dimpled smile. She should have been in a church choir, not on stage shouting about racial prejudice and nuclear holocaust, especially since there was no longer any prejudice or nuclear bombs. Eric had once asked Sammy what he liked about her, and Sammy had said he was still working on the computer program that would tell him. Like Strem, her attraction was her energy, but unlike him, she worked too hard trying to get it across. A life-threatening interstellar journey was probably just what she needed to settle her down.

"Hello, Strem," Cleo responded sweetly. "How many years are we going to get on Mercury for this?"

"Let's discuss that when we're all together," Sammy said, obviously concerned about who might be listening. "You'll be here soon."

Soon was twenty minutes later. Eric was grateful she hadn't brought her serpent, though her quarter-ton suitcase of costumes and makeup might have unlooked-for surprises inside it. Her dress was unusually conservative, a pink plastic pantsuit dotted with tiny purple spiders, and her hair was its natural red color. He was

mildly curious how a pair of opants would respond to
her legs.

"Give me a kiss," Cleo commanded Sammy, draping
her arms around him and plopping in his lap as he sat
before his controls. He managed to obey while keeping
an eye glued to his screens. Cleo nuzzled her nose
against his ear. "I missed you, honey," she said.

"You saw me three days ago."

"Didn't you miss me?"

"To a degree, I suppose." You couldn't fault Sammy
for his honesty.

Cleo stood, slightly offended, and turned to Strem.
"Give me a real hug, would you, big boy?" Strem was
quick to oblige. Jeanie and Cleo even exchanged a brief
embrace. The risk they were taking might have been
responsible for the tenderness. Normally Jeanie and
Cleo moved in separate social circles and were not very
close. Cleo even squeezed Eric hello and he squeezed
her back.

Sammy requested and received permission to leave
orbit. Mars went the way of Earth, seemingly falling
into a bottomless hole. What was different this time was
their direction in relationship to the plane of the solar
system. They were not heading out toward Jupiter and
Saturn, but were arcing "upward" (figuratively speaking, there is no up and down in space) where the
planets never traveled.

As the empty miles grew into numbers the human
mind could not properly grasp, and the sun shrank and
faded, their chatter began to die down. The vastness of
the space around them began to cast its spell. The five
of them stared silently out the windows, each in his or
her way trying to comprehend the incomprehensible,
the possibility that they might soon be "out there."

Eric teetered on a narrow strip of joy and uncer-

tainty. Yet, beneath the conflicting emotions, he had a
quiet feeling that he was about to reach a point in his
life he had waited a long time to meet. He was unable
to fully explain the intuition, or shake it, and it grew
stronger the longer he looked at the stars.

Even traveling at a third of the speed of light,
Excalibur needed roughly twelve hours to reach Central Control's Customs Line. When Strem suggested
taking a nap, Eric thought it would be impossible to
sleep not knowing whether they were going to make
history or end up with criminal records. But when the
others greeted the suggestion with approval—except for
Sammy, who could not be pried from the controls—he
decided to give it a try and headed for his quarters, a
sparse cubicle that had not been designed for the
claustrophobic.

Turning off the light and lying down, the tightness in
his neck and the pressure beneath his eyes began to
flow out of Eric as if he had just drunk from a narcotic
draught. The silent sense that he was about to cross a
line drawn by destiny persisted and began to weave
rich images as he started to doze. He saw swelling stars
that were far older than the sun, consuming in a few
violent hours the reserves of a fuel supply that had
lasted many eons. And arid planets where people walked
that were not really people at all, but beings evolved
out of seas that had centuries ago dried on winds that
no longer blew. Of course he often dreamed of the
unknown, and surely whatever lay beyond The Tachyon
Web would remain unknown, and never think of him.

And so Eric fell asleep.

3

Excalibur was stopped dead in space. The sun was an overly bright star, nothing more, and The Milky Way was a wide river of a billion softly blended stars. They were literally hundreds of millions of miles away from another human being. Yet, they were being watched. Central Control had noted their passage out of the solar system and wanted to have a talk with Uncle Dan.

"It'll work, right?" Strem asked Sammy, who had not left his seat, not even to go to the bathroom, since boarding. Sammy rolled his tired head around and looked up at Strem with his usual emotionless expression.

"I seem to remember you telling me it couldn't fail."

"You're the scientist, dammit," Strem complained. "Tell me it will work so that I can relax."

Sammy turned back to the console. His fingers danced over a keyboard and a two-foot miniature of Strem's uncle, dressed in a trader's traditional red suit and perfect in every observable detail, suddenly appeared in the holographic cubical. The image was for their reference only. Uncle Dan's full form was being piped out on a tachyon band directly to Central Control. The authorities would perceive him as standing on an otherwise empty deck. "I wouldn't relax," Sammy said.

"When will the Customs Officer begin?" Eric asked. His nap had lasted three hours and he was now wide awake. He'd been working on an ulcer all week and now, at the moment of truth, he felt inexplicably confident. But he would be glad when it was all over.

"Soon," Sammy said. "Very soon."

"This suspense is great," Cleo said, sitting beside Sammy. Eric couldn't help noticing how her high-heeled feet tapped restlessly on the floor.

"How can you say that?" Jeanie asked. Her opants were a dirty purple, streaked with every imaginable color. In other words, she was ready for a nervous breakdown. Strem hugged her, and she rested her head on his shoulder, sighing. "Why couldn't we just go to the moon like normal kids?"

"Leave it to me to show a girl an exciting time," Strem said gamely.

"Don't worry, Jeanie," Cleo said. "My aunt is a fantastic lawyer. She can make it look in court as though it were all Strem's fault."

"Leave it to me to pick a loyal crew," Strem said.

"Here it comes," Sammy said.

Central Control's symbol, two overlapping triangles with a dot in the center, appeared on the screen. Sammy typed in *Excalibur*'s code number, her destination, and expected return date. Eric knew this information was being cross-referenced with the information Uncle Dan had given aboard Space Station One. In a moment the preliminaries were over. The symbol faded, and a wrinkly old customs agent, wearing a featureless white turtleneck uniform, came on the screen. Though his tiny head and obviously thin frame gave him a birdlike fragility, his voice was firm and authoritative. It was fortunate that they could see him and he couldn't see them.

"Mr. Daniel Hark, a pleasure to see you again so soon. Business must be prosperous."

"Damn," Strem breathed. "He knows him."

"Perhaps," Sammy said, glancing at the holographic model, which leaned forward as though trying to see the customs agent better.

Was this a test here at the very beginning? Eric wondered.

"Forgive me, sir," Uncle Dan's recording said. "You have the advantage. Business has been so busy I've forgotten your name."

"My name is Jeret Queenshear. And I'm the one who must apologize, I mistook you for someone else. We've never met." It had definitely been a test. Jeret continued, "Have you been to the Tau Ceti System before?"

"A number of times." The responses were intentionally brief so as not to invite further questions.

"Ah, yes." Jeret nodded, glancing downward. "I see you were there only last December."

"Last January," Daniel Hark corrected automatically. Eric was impressed with the thoroughness of Sammy's preparation. As the responses had obviously not been recorded in succession, to move smoothly from one to the next was quite a feat.

"Are you aware of the ban Tau Ceti has placed on the importation of drugs otherwise allowed in The Union?"

"On Bromitzen and Quibzen, yes. I have neither aboard."

"What is the anticipated credit transference relating to your cargo?"

"Fifty-five thousand, approximately."

"When was *Excalibur*'s last inspection?"

"Last week. It's there in your records."

"So it is. How many passengers have you aboard?"

Sammy lost his slouch, suddenly sitting up. "We've got a problem," he said quickly.

"Five," the holograph answered.

"Their names, please?" Jeret asked.

"What is it?" Strem demanded.

"I am not obligated to supply you with their names."

"Agreed, but we would prefer it if you would. For our records, you understand."

"He'll want to see us," Sammy said. We'll have to go on manual and improvise."

"Oh, no. Don't." Strem groaned. Cleo jumped to her feet and her carefully crafted tough image stayed seated. Jeanie's opants appeared to overload and went blank. Eric felt his heart rate double and his self-confidence slashed in half. If they had to pause to think what to advise the holograph to say, even for a couple of seconds, Central Control would get suspicious. Eric moved closer to Sammy and his console.

"I don't understand," Uncle Dan retorted. "Their identity is confidential under Section A of Senate Amendment Twenty-seven. We are in free space."

Jeret nodded with a trace of impatience. "We are aware of the law. Still, the request is not unreasonable. We simply want to make sure your passengers are comfortable. May we at least see them?"

"We cannot give another stall," Sammy said with grave certainty. Laws and amendments aside, Jeret could haul them in if he felt like it. Eric acted without thinking, which often worked better for him.

"Go to manual!" he ordered Sammy. "Say, he'd have to wake us."

Sammy did not hesitate. He activated his mike and said, "I'd have to wake them."

"I'd have to wake them," Uncle Dan said.

"All of them?" Jeret asked.

Eric crowded Sammy aside. "Let me see," he said directly into the mike.

"Let me see," Uncle Dan said.

"Very well," Jeret nodded.

Eric disengaged the mike. "Have him walk away!"

"No problem," Sammy said, typing vigorously on the computer keyboard. The holograph strolled out of its cubical area and vanished. As far as Jeret was concerned, Daniel Hark had just left the bridge.

"Now what?" Strem said. "Why did you tell Jeret that?"

"I was buying us time," Eric said.

"For what?" Strem demanded.

"What would you have done?" Eric yelled back.

"Don't fight!" Jeanie pleaded.

"Can we tell them it was all just a joke?" Cleo asked in a small voice.

"Let's have less talk and more thought," Sammy said, and even he sounded slightly exasperated. "We have at most a minute to figure out what to do next."

"You're the genius!" Strem told Sammy. "You do the thinking!"

"We could have Daniel Hark tell him that none of us will get up," Sammy muttered.

"That would make Jeret suspicious," Eric said, frowning in concentration, feeling the seconds slip away. Time—it was always there except when you needed it.

"We would be on weak ground," Sammy agreed.

"Could your aunt also represent me?" Strem asked Cleo.

Eric looked at Sammy, into his brilliant bloodshot eyes, and saw no magic solution forthcoming. On the screen Jeret had turned to the side and was talking to someone they couldn't see. For a moment Eric was tempted to recommend they attempt an illegal hyper jump. But that would be sheer madness. They would only stall immediately outside the solar system's web. It was only when he began to despair that a possibility came to him. "Can we overlap a view of the bridge as it is now with the phony one we are transmitting?"

Sammy nodded reluctantly. "Yes, but there will be discrepancies. We have lights and systems on that we didn't have on when we filmed Strem's uncle. We won't have time to match everything. Also, we would have to interact with Daniel Hark, and that could get sticky. We can change his words but the program necessarily takes care of most of his movements. You've seen how he goes all over the place. If he were to step through one of us—"

"Do it!" Strem barked. "There's no other choice. We'll stay near the edges of the room."

Sammy turned back to his computer. "I'll erase the image in our holograph at least. It wouldn't do to have Jeret see that."

And that would make it that much harder to stay out of Daniel Hart's way, Eric thought. He tried to focus on simplifying things. "Two of us will be enough to convince Jeret the passengers are safe," he said, after a moment's consideration.

"You're right," Strem said. "Which two?"

"I'll be talking for your uncle," Sammy said, working frantically to complete the setup. "Count me out."

"I'm not good at talking to people that aren't there," Jeanie said, trembling where she stood.

"Cleo and I will greet Jeret," Eric said with absolutely no enthusiasm. "We are both dressed as if we could have been in bed." It was true the two of them had changed into sweats, but that was only part of the reason for wanting Cleo over Strem. She was a performing singer, used to acting in front of others. She should be able to play a simple straight role.

"You mean, in bed together?" Strem winced.

Eric ignored him and studied Cleo. Her eyes wavered and she paled but then she shrugged and forced a smile. "It's just another stage to me," she said, trying to sound nonchalant. "Where do I stand?"

"We will come in from off deck," Eric said, "following Uncle Dan. Can that be arranged?"

"Yes," Sammy said momentarily withdrawing his hands from the keyboard, flexing his fingers like an athlete before the final quarter. "It's ready." He nodded to Jeanie and Strem. "You two get off deck and don't make a sound."

"Won't Jeret be able to hear you telling Uncle Dan what to say?" Strem asked Sammy, leading Jeanie to the hall adjacent to the sleeping quarters. Eric guided Cleo to the corner of the bridge.

"No," Sammy said. "I'll fluctuate the audio reception. And yes, I know Jeret might notice the fluctuations. One thing, Eric and Cleo—if I should wave you in a certain direction, just move. I still have a visual of Daniel Hark on my screen." Sammy checked his indicators one last time. "Get set. Come only a third of the way into the room. Ready?"

"Yes," Eric answered for both of them. He wished he were at home and bored.

Sammy waved them forward. Eric told his legs to move and was glad they were still able to hear him. Cleo followed a pace behind. He could hear her rapid breathing and worried that she was hyperventilating. Sammy slowly turned a dial next to his microphone.

"I managed to fetch two of them," Sammy said. "The others are out cold."

The identical statements were repeated by a disembodied Daniel Hark. Jeret nodded as though that were satisfactory and looked at them. He smiled, an expression he probably kept reserved for people eighteen and under. "Your names, please?" he asked.

"I'm Eric Tirel." There was a forever pause. Cleo was having trouble remembering her name. Eric took the initiative. "And this is Cleo Rettson. You wished to speak to us, sir?"

"I wanted to be sure that your passage is a comfortable one. Central is sensitive to the travel of youngsters in interstellar space."

"We're having a wonderful time!" Cleo said, too loud and too enthusiastically.

Jeret smiled again and he was lucky his stiff face didn't crack. "How about you, Mr. Tirel?"

"The trip has been very exciting so far," Eric said honestly. Keep it short and simple, he thought. But an expression on Jeret's face prodded him to speak again and speak quickly. Something on the bridge was disturbing the customs man, probably a slight change in the coloration of a couple of lights caused by the overlay. "Do you know, sir, how long it will be before we can make our hyper jump to Tau Ceti?"

The question got Jeret's attention back. He blinked twice and rubbed his eyes. "Once you receive clearance," he said, "it should take only a few minutes to reach the jump point. That is, if Mr. Hark taxis out immediately." Jeret paused to give Daniel Hark a chance to respond but Sammy chose to play it silent. A glance at Sammy told Eric why. Sammy was frantically gesturing Cleo and him to move to the left. Eric did so automatically, as casually as he could, and promptly banged into Cleo, practically knocking her over. He caught her just as Jeret asked, "Are you having trouble with your stabilizers?"

"No," Sammy and Daniel Hark said. "The ship is fine. You made me wake them so quickly, it's no wonder they're bumping into each other."

"If possible, sir," Eric said, "we'd like to get another hour's rest before the jump."

"We're anxious to return to bed," Cleo said in a high, excited voice, clasping his hand for what reason Eric did not know. Jeret interpreted her to mean the young nasty brats were anxious to return to bed for activities other than rest. It was funny in a way, for now he was the one who wanted the conversation to come to an end.

"I see," he said dryly. "I thank you for your time." Eric nodded and swished Cleo offstage to where Strem was grinning idiotically and Jeanie was biting her nails. Now it was in Sammy's hands.

Jeret continued, "I think it would be safe to say those two are not aboard against their will." He cleared his throat. "How you run your ship, Mr. Hark, is your business." Jeret nodded to a person or persons offscreen. "You have been cleared for a jump to the Tau Ceti System. Please proceed out an additional ten million miles before initiating the jump. For all of Central, I wish you a safe and profitable trip."

"Thank you," Sammy and Mr. Hark responded. Jeret disappeared and was replaced for an instant by Central Control's triangular symbol. Then that too vanished and Strem started howling like a wolf at the moon. Eric couldn't see the smile on his own face but could feel its tips brushing his earlobes. Especially when Cleo gave him a tight hug and Jeanie planted a warm kiss on his lips.

"We did it!" Strem raised his clenched fists.

"Sammy and Eric did it," Jeanie said, laughing, softening her remark by embracing her boyfriend. "Face it, you and I just got in the way."

"My pet brain," Cleo crooned, sitting in Sammy's lap, actually petting his long brown hair. Sammy did not mind. He was smiling and Sammy had not really smiled since he had learned to read.

"Eric is the one who took control," he said. "I was drawing blanks left and right when Jeret started in on us."

"Let's hear it for Eric!" Jeanie applauded, the others giving him a standing ovation. The hero worship was overdone and silly and that made Eric enjoy it all the more.

"Eric did such a fine job," Cleo said mischievously as the commotion died down, "I think he should be our leader instead of Strem."

"Wait a second," Strem said. "Didn't I just demonstrate what a great leader I am?" No one answered him with a quick affirmative. "But what is a leader if he doesn't know when to delegate responsibility?"

"I don't want to be captain," Eric said easily. The atmosphere was so light and festive that he was surprised when Strem glanced at Sammy—the two catching each other's eyes—and said seriously:

"You better believe you don't, buddy."

The short line dropped like a weight on the deck, pulling them all down with it. Jeanie turned to Cleo, who frowned, bewildered. "What?" Eric said softly.

Strem shook his head, all business, and strode to the

dark windows, turning his back on them. "Take us to the jump point, Sammy," he ordered.

Sammy let go of Cleo and moved to activate the holographic cube. The three-dimensional projection now encompassed a much larger field, filled with stars rather than planets. The diffused gravitational pulls of the widely separated suns were represented by hazy red bands that rippled around the bright pinpoints like cool fog around unflickering candles. A white line pierced the mist, connecting two stars. It was to be their path through hyper space.

"Cleo was only joking," Eric said, coming up beside Strem, afraid he had offended his friend. He was confused. Strem got upset about as often as a bench complained about being sat on.

"No, I wasn't," Cleo said.

"Here comes the exciting part," Strem said, a disturbing glint in his eye. He had not even heard them. Eric was reminded of his sudden seriousness at the observation tower in Baja. His manner then was identical to now. What had triggered it then? There was a word on the tip of Eric's tongue, but he couldn't remember.

"We've had enough excitement for one day," Eric said. *Excalibur* began to hum and the lights flickered as Sammy activated the graviton drive. They would be in position to jump in a minute. And suddenly Eric's suspicion that Strem was hiding a crucial fact became a certainty, even before Strem spoke.

"Eric," he said, with something akin to regret in his face, "don't think I didn't trust you. I did. But . . . I wanted it to be a surprise."

"Did I miss something somewhere?" Cleo muttered.

"Strem?" Jeanie said, worried.

"A nova," Eric whispered, the word coming back to him.

"Approaching the required coordinates," Sammy said.

"How long?" Strem asked, leaning his head on the window, momentarily closing his eyes. He looked scared, and jubilant, and Eric didn't know which was worse.

"Fifteen seconds," Sammy said. "Fourteen . . . Twelve . . . Ten . . ."

Eric shook Strem. Standing so close to the tall window, it was as though the two of them could take a step forward and fall forever. Eric did not want to take that step.

"We're not going to Tau Ceti, are we?" he asked. Strem did not answer. Eric grabbed him by the collar and yanked him around. "*Are we?*"

"Eight . . . Seven . . . Six. . . . We don't have to do it," Sammy said, and the remark was more frightening than any of Jeret's questions.

Strem smiled faintly. "You're right, Eric. You're a smart guy. I knew you'd figure it out. You've read about how much energy novas put out—they short-circuit anything nearby." He turned toward Sammy and nodded. "Do it!"

"*Where are we going?*" Eric shouted.

Too late—it was done. *Excalibur*'s hyper drive turned on. As time did not exist in hyper space as it did in the relative universe, the marvelous mechanism was on and off in the same instant. Nevertheless, the human mind has thoughts and feelings that come and go without the tiniest tick of the clock. Eric had the sensation of stepping outside himself and turning around and finding that he was still in the same place. There was no light in the interdimensional abyss but neither was there darkness, and he suffered from neither heat nor cold.

Still, emotions often care nothing for the surroundings. His disorientation chased the skipped light years like a meteor through the nighttime sky. When the blink of time and space was complete, and the rays of an exploding sun flooded the bridge with an unbearable glare, Eric repeated his question, minus one word.

"Where are we?"

Strem threw his arm over his eyes and tried to look through the window. "We're outside," he said. "We've jumped beyond The Tachyon Web."

4

The cosmic inferno bombarding *Excalibur* disallowed
even a chance of disbelief; the pieces fit together in a
moment for Eric. They had not jumped toward Tau
Ceti. The cargo run had been a ruse. Instead, they'd
leapt into the Andromeda Sector, next to the nova,
where the disintegrating star must have torn a hole in
The Tachyon Web, a hole they had plunged through.

Strem had risked their lives without telling them and
that should have made Eric furious. As Eric backed
away from the window, though, trying to shield his
eyes and still take in the galactic spectacle, his anger
was all but drowned in a momentous wave of awe. They
were *outside*. They could go *anywhere*. He bumped
into a chair and sat down.

"Raise the window filters!" Strem yelled.

"They're up," Sammy replied.

Eric's pupils were adjusting, painfully. The forward
window was no longer a featureless mass of light. A
blue-white star burned in the center and either it was
incredibly huge or else it was way too close. Sweat

beaded onto his forehead. The cabin temperature was rising rapidly.

"They must be broken," Strem said, moving toward the control console, his body seemingly afire, aurora blazing round his limbs.

"I don't think so," Sammy said, practically invisible, sitting as he was to the side of the windows, outside the path of the harsh rays. Eric couldn't even find Cleo and Jeanie. "But I can't read my indicators."

"Put the shields down," Eric said. His eyes ached and he had to close them.

"It sure is a bright bastard," Strem breathed. "Take us out of here!"

"Strem," Jeanie whispered.

"In a moment," Strem said. "Sammy, how are we doing?"

"I'm not sure. But the ship's hot. Very hot."

Then they heard a hiss. For an instant Eric thought Cleo had misled them, that she had in fact brought her python.

The hiss was coming from his back, to the left. He cracked one eye and saw nothing but light. Then the sound turned to a screeching whistle, and the bridge was flooded with a gas that looked and felt as though it were lava.

Eric leapt to his feet. "Close the shields!" he yelled again. The shields were external panels that could slip over the windows. They wouldn't stop the gas, but at least they would block the glare and give them a chance to see and deal with the problem.

The girls started to panic. One of them, Eric couldn't tell which one, banged into him as he stumbled toward the windows. He fell and struck his head on a pipe, pain flaring from the base of his skull into his neck. With the scalding steam, the skin on his face and hands felt ready to blister. Chemical fumes stuffed his nostrils, irritating his lungs, making him cough.

"We're losing our coolant!" Sammy shouted.

"Stop it!" Strem shouted back.

"How?" Sammy asked.

Eric pulled himself up and felt his way along the forward window, his arms up and searching. A glimpse outside showed a staggering incandescent shell of violet plasma, stretching away from them in every direction, encircling the nova, and through which *Excalibur* was undoubtedly rushing.

The whine of the graviton drive mixed with the scream of the steam. Eric wondered if Sammy hadn't confused their direction and wasn't racing them toward a fiery end. Eric's fingers found the manual shield control above the rim of the windows, and he depressed it firmly. The hull vibrated as the external panels slid into place. The cry of the escaping coolant soared through the octaves, piercing his ears.

As the shields snapped shut, the bridge should have been visible under the normal lighting conditions. But their eyes had overdosed on light. A dim blurred gray enveloped the cabin. The boiling gas continued its inhuman ravings for a moment more, then cut off in a frightening silence, leaving them with pounding hearts, ragged breaths. Eric blinked at the swirling mist that thwarted his vision, not knowing if it was the steam or his sizzled irises.

"I have turned our vents to maximum," Sammy said finally. "The gas should be gone in a minute or two."

Hazy colored dots peaked out of the gloom. The bridge took on rough dimension. Eric watched as Strem shuffled slowly toward Jeanie and took her hands. She was crying but getting hold of herself. Cleo lay sprawled on the floor near the hyper drive. Eric realized it had been she he had struck in his rush to the window. He helped her up and she nodded her thanks before launching into a coughing fit.

The ship's atmosphere was oppressively hot and humid. The coolant odor, however, was diminishing rapidly. Sammy had removed his shirt and was wiping the control console. Eric put a hand to the back of his head and felt a bloody bump. Perhaps two minutes had passed since they had made the jump. It was hard to believe.

"Are we moving?" Eric asked Sammy.

"Yes." Sammy pressed his face against a foggy screen. "We have point-one-eight the velocity of light away from the nova." He consulted another indicator beside a flashing red button. "And we no longer have any coolant circulating around our Preeze Cap."

"Is that what keeps us from overheating?" Cleo asked, her voice exceptionally high and unsteady.

"The Preeze Cap cools the Hial Diffusor," Sammy explained. "Which in turn cools *Excalibur*'s drives."

"It's the same difference," Eric muttered, feeling unsteady on his feet. "How long can we keep the graviton drive on?"

"Except for the components that generate our protective force field, I've already shut it down," Sammy said. "We have substantial speed. Had I tried for more we might have blown up."

"But are we still generating excess heat?" Eric asked.

"Yes. Slowly."

"Couldn't we turn off the force field and just let all the machinery cool down?" Strem asked.

"This close to the nova," Sammy replied, "nothing's going to cool down. And without the field we'd vaporize in a fraction of a second. Even when we get further away we have to keep it up. At our speed a collision with a stray particle the size of a pea would finish us."

Eric wiped at the sweat stinging his sore eyes. "Can we make a jump?"

"Not without coolant for the Preeze Cap," Sammy said.

Eric was not sure if anyone else realized it, but Sammy had pretty much just said they were goners. They would find no coolant this side of The Tachyon Web. His anger quickened. He looked at Strem through the sober light.

"It's a long story," Strem said.

"You said *that* at the spaceport," Eric snapped. "Looks like we'll have plenty of time to hear it." His sight continued to improve, to the point where he could see Jeanie's lips quivering.

"Are we in trouble?" Jeanie whispered.

"Ask your brave boyfriend," Eric grumbled.

Strem let go of Jeanie and began to pace in front of the closed windows. A cool draft started to blow from the direction of the sleeping quarters.

"Let's not panic," Strem said. "We're still in one piece. Nobody's been hurt. We have plenty of options."

He glanced at Sammy, who shrugged, as if to say: don't ask me to list them. "That we've come this far is quite an accomplishment in itself," Strem continued. "I would think you, Eric, of all people, would be impressed."

Eric didn't answer. He was thinking that when it came time to ration their food and water, he was taking Strem's share.

"*Where* are we?" Cleo finally asked. "What's this about being outside the web? No one can go outside the web."

"Hull temperature has dropped slightly," Sammy said.

"Good," Strem said. "See? Things are looking up already."

"And there is a growing instability in our force field," Sammy added.

"Will it hold?" Eric asked.

"Interesting question," Sammy murmured.

All eyes turned to Strem. Perspiration had stained the contours of his thick muscles through his shirt, but his foul-up deprived him of the image of strength. He leaned against the covered windows, then jumped back upright, having apparently singed his shoulder blades. So much for the hull temperature dropping.

"As I was saying," Strem went on, "what we have accomplished will be remembered. We're the first civilians to get outside the web. We're—"

"Spare us the historical perspective," Eric interrupted, moving toward the draft, plopping down on the floor against a wall that wasn't doubling as a frying pan. The fumes were practically gone. He began to believe his eyes might once again work normally.

"Eric, you're bleeding," Jeanie said, also having been drawn in the direction of the cool air. She stood above him, pointing to the back of his head.

"Don't worry, nobody's been hurt," he said sarcastically. "Strem, you can start explaining now."

"It was Sammy's idea." He smiled. "That's a joke." No one laughed. Strem sighed. "Actually, it was Sammy's brother who first brought up the possibility. All of you know Lien Balan does technical work for people in high places. He heard about the nova, or I should say, the impending nova. Earth's astronomers have known for months this star was going to explode—almost to the day of when it was going to happen. Anyway, one evening Lien let Sammy and me in on the discovery. The information was not strictly classified. The Patrol probably hadn't figured the nova as a military threat. On the other hand, Lien didn't want us telling others about it. He was talking way above me, and maybe even above Sammy, but we both got the clear impression that the energy put out by the nova would disrupt The Tachyon Web in this sector."

"Did Lien suggest you try to jump out?" Eric asked.

"Not exactly," Strem admitted. "For him, it was more of an interesting theoretical possibility."

"You took us on this insane ride all on the basis of an interesting theoretical possibility?" Eric said.

Strem spoke quickly. "Lien was confident of his calculations. Wasn't he, Sammy?"

Sammy had his scraggy face tucked inside an opened panel beneath his console. Not less than seven indicators were blinking red alert. "Lien's always confident of his calculations," he mumbled.

"Is Lien that guy I met at your house that I thought was an android?" Cleo asked Sammy.

"That was my brother."

"Does Uncle Dan know about this?" Eric asked.

Strem chuckled. "Are you crazy?"

"You're the last one who should be allowed to ask that," Eric said.

"My uncle would risk anything for a buck, but he wouldn't lay out a cent to satisfy even his curiosity. Sammy and I figured we could get out here, look around for a day or two, and still make the delivery in time."

"Looks as if the delivery is going to be late," Eric muttered.

"I know what you're thinking," Strem began.

"You don't!" Eric shot back. "How could you when you obviously didn't know what *you* were thinking when you planned this disaster? The Preeze Cap is melting as we talk. Sure, we might be able to get far enough out to where we won't be turned to ash when our force field quits on us, but then what? We can't make a jump.

We're in the middle of nowhere. How long will our supplies last? Two weeks? A month, at the most? Admit it, Strem, you blew it. For all of us."

For the first time since he'd known him, Strem had no ready answer. He glanced at Jeanie, for whom the truth was slowly sinking in, then at the floor. Cleo went to stand beside Sammy, who broke from his repair job to share the gloom with them. Minutes went by without words. Suddenly, Jeanie turned and left, reappearing a moment later with a first aid kit. She began to dab at Eric's bump with a sterilized pad and a stinging solution, crying quietly.

Eric felt a stab of guilt. He'd always thought of himself as the cool one under pressure. Perhaps there were options. He caught Jeanie's wrist, squeezed it gently, and said, "It's all right." Jeanie held his eyes for a second, then nodded and tried to smile. Eric patted her on the side and, taking a deep breath of the still warm air, stood up.

"The vents sucked up the ethylene glycol," he said. "Where did they put it?"

"The coolant would have been trapped by the atmosphere filtration system," Sammy replied.

Strem showed signs of life. "I'll take you to it. Do you think we can reclaim some of the fluid?"

"Let's see," Eric said.

Strem led him into the cargo bay. Eric was surprised with its size, even with the crowding cartons of opants. The air was cooler here, of both tension and temperature. Soft yellow light spilled from the ceiling. Eric's head began to clear. As Strem led him along a narrow corridor made up of stacked boxes, Eric stopped him.

"You should have told us," he said.

Strem nodded, properly chastised. "I know."

"Our chances are lousy."

"I wouldn't want to bet on them," Strem agreed.

"But it was a daring idea. It took a lot of imagination."

Strem's face brightened. "It was my idea. I thought to myself, how many times do we have a nova go off next to the web? It was a chance I couldn't pass up. I just wanted my friends with me to enjoy the excitement. Neither Sammy nor I thought we'd come out so close to the blasted star."

"I understand."

"You don't hate me?"

"Not intensely."

The twin man-height filtration barrels attached to the corner of the bay opened easily, and they found the coolant, all forty gallons of it, impregnated in two of the filthiest filters either of them had ever had the displeasure to smell. Apparently, over the last twenty years, Uncle Dan had transported tons of toxic solutions in less than perfectly sealed containers. Plus, Strem added, while traveling, his uncle smoked the nastiest cigars. Whatever had been in *Excalibur*'s air during all those trips was now mixed in with the ethylene glycol.

"Isn't there some regulation about changing these filters annually?" Eric asked. They were standing on a crate of opants, holding their noses.

"Yes, but I guess it's not strictly enforced." Strem replaced the lids. "So what do you think?"

"We have no idea what could be in these barrels that could have dissolved in the coolant. But it doesn't really matter, in a way. We're still going to have to try to purify the stuff."

"What are we going to use to filter it?"

"We'll find something."

*   *   *

The girls joined in the search for a suitable material to rid the coolant of the gook. The work provided a positive distraction. Jeanie and Cleo even got the impression, thanks to Strem's optimistic explanation, that they were practically half way home. They went through everything: bed sheets, carpets, pillows.

Several hours later, the girls finally discovered the key ingredient to their envisioned chemical factory: the inner lining of the opant jackets was made of a silklike material. When they poured a cup of the polluted coolant through it, the coolant came out the other side a shade less foul. But there were two difficulties. One, the ethylene glycol penetrated the material slowly. A glass of the liquid poured atop the inside of one jacket seeped through at only a couple of drops a minute. Also, when Sammy took a look at the end product, he said there was no way he was putting it near the Preeze Cap. The coolant was going to have to pass through many layers of the material if it was to stand a chance of performing.

Eric decided to go back to the bridge. He left Strem working to siphon the contaminated fluid into pails while the girls hacked dozens of opant jackets to pieces. When he arrived, Eric found Sammy glued to his computers.

"Any new developments?" Eric asked.

Sammy looked up cheerfully. The crisis hadn't dented his equanimity. Although the cabin temperature had returned to normal, he had yet to put his shirt back on. "I've been searching for planets," he said.

"To hide behind? Wouldn't we just overheat trying to stop?"

"Yes, we would. I was simply curious to see if there were any. So far, I've located three gaseous giants and one Earth-size world. There may be more."

Eric felt a chill up his spine. Images of vast oceans turning to mountains of steam, of green forests being swept up in hurricanes of ash came unbidden, bringing with them an unreasonable sense of loss. "Could there have been life on any of them?" he asked.

"Unlikely. A star that goes nova isn't fine one day and then ready to explode the next. For at least the last hundred years, the conditions on the Earth-size world must have been too severe to support life."

"I suppose you're right." Eric strode to the closed windows. "Are we far enough out to have another look at it?"

"I think so. We're out about the same distance that Uranus is from our sun." Sammy pressed a switch. The shields protested for a moment with loud scrapes— partially jammed due to the excessive heat—before sliding free. Without the pressure of being blinded and scalded to death, they were both able to appreciate the sight, and for a bit, Eric forgot their predicament.

It was a jeweler's masterpiece. A blazing sapphire set in rings of amethysts, emeralds, and topazes; the nova in the center, encircled by shells of plasma and gas glowing with different portions of the spectrum: violets, greens, yellows—the cooler bands situated the furthest from the ferocious sun. The Earth's sun, viewed from the same distance, would have been a bright star. If Sammy were to lift the filters, they wouldn't even be able to look out the window.

"It's beautiful," Eric whispered finally.

"It's a shame we're the only ones who can see it like this," Sammy agreed.

"I've been thinking, maybe we're not. There are no civilian pilots out here. What about The Patrol?"

"They could have brought astronomers into this region," Sammy said thoughtfully. "But tachyon transmissions are totally drowned out around here. That is, of course, the reason Lien knew the web would be inoperative in this sector." He paused. "Do we even want to try to contact The Patrol?"

"If it's a choice between dying."

"They might be able to find us, if they were looking for us, but I doubt we could find them."

"We could broadcast an SOS on regular electromagnetic frequencies."

"They would have to be close, real close, to pick it up in the reasonable future."

"I think we should try it," Eric said.

"I'd have to discuss it with Strem first."

"I think he'll go for it when he starts to get hungry." Eric turned his back to the nova and leaned against the window. "What went wrong, Sammy?"

"First, Strem's uncle did not replace the seal on the Preeze Cap like he said he did. Then the energy that allowed us to pierce the web distorted our hyper plot. We were lucky we didn't come out of the jump inside the nova."

"I guess we should be thankful for small favors."

Sammy looked unhappy. "I told Strem to let you in on the scheme. He was afraid you wouldn't come, that you would miss all the fun." He glanced at the drive temperature indicator. "But with the way things have turned out, I guess that wouldn't have been such a bad thing."

Eric smiled and lied. "Knowing what I do now, I probably still would have come."

They enjoyed the nova a while longer and then Eric left to work on the filter. He was in for a surprise. Once he outlined the simple design to the others—the linings of the opant jackets were to be sewn together in groups of four and suspended by interlaced cords, hammock fashion, above one of the ship's bathtubs—they no longer needed him. The girls could handle the stitching and Strem told Eric that since there was only one pail for hauling the dirty coolant to the bathroom, he would just get in his way. Eric could see it was important for the three of them to stay busy and didn't protest. Besides, he was hungry.

He left the haphazard operation, went to the galley, and ate more than any marooned passenger had a right to. The heavy meal made him drowsy, and when Sammy refused to be relieved from the helm, he once again found himself in his own room, staring at the ceiling. He did not remember closing his eyes and dozing off.

Someone was shaking him. He sat up and opened his eyes, taking a startled breath. Bare-chested, Sammy was sitting on his bed, the others standing at his back with the strangest looks on their faces. Where he was came back to him in an instant.

"How long have I been out?"

"Two hours," Strem said.

"You let me sleep two hours?" Everyone kept staring at him. "What is it?"

"We have some bad news and some bizarre news," Strem said.

"We have filtered five gallons of the coolant," Sammy said. "Something must be dissolved in it."

"How can you tell?"

"It still stinks," Sammy said. "But we haven't given up on it." He paused, cleared his throat. "We're picking up transmissions on several electromagnetic frequencies, lightspeed. Their source is nearby."

"So The Patrol is out here after all," Eric muttered.

Sammy shook his head. "These transmissions don't belong to us, to any of us."

"What do you mean?"

"They're not of human origin," Sammy said.

5

They were gathered on the bridge. Eric had not pinched himself but he had drunk a cup of coffee and knew he was not dreaming. Yet the enchanting light of the nova and its prismatic halos—further away for the last two hours of travel, but still overwhelming—had the control room aglow with such etheric hues that it was easy to believe his mind was still wandering in a fantasy universe created by his unconscious. Sammy was explaining, matter-of-factly, how he had made the greatest discovery in human history.

"I was scanning for a flux of a graviton drive, searching for a Patrol cruiser, when I came across a powerful stream of high-velocity ions. At first, I thought it was some type of natural phenomenon triggered by the nova, perhaps a comet's reaction to the high radiation. Then I got this strange feeling. I'd seen this type of stream before."

"Didn't primitive spacecraft used to be propelled by accelerated particles?" Eric asked.

Sammy nodded. "It was one of the methods used

before the discovery of the graviton drive. That's why I recognized it. I'd seen it on history videos. But never on a scale such as this. I still didn't think the phenomenon could be artificial until I focused *Excalibur*'s main dish on it. Then I started to pick up this."

Sammy activated the holographic cube in the center of the bridge. The image was cracked with static but was nevertheless sufficiently clear to steal Eric's breath away. It was a man and it wasn't a man. His features were femininely soft, his skin smooth and golden, partially hidden beneath a bush of curly white hair. None of these qualities would have gotten him stopped on the street back on Earth. But his perfectly round whiteless eyes, dark green centers set in light green sockets, would have made him a standout at one of Cleo's punk parties.

The man was slightly built, clothed in a loose blue tunic that fastened at the neck with a silver clasp. His incomprehensible words were soft and musical, especially in comparison to the flat tones of English, the only language spoken on Earth. Eric took an immediate liking to him.

"Could the interference be causing a color distortion?" he asked.

"This is his actual appearance," Sammy said confidently.

Cleo squealed with delight. "He's a doll! What's his name?"

"She'll want his phone number next," Strem remarked. "He's an alien, Cleo. How do you know he doesn't drink blood for lunch?"

Jeanie laughed. "I think Strem's jealous."

"What are we watching?" Eric asked. He had swallowed piercing the web, getting fried by a nova, and even his possible death. But aliens were going to take time, maybe the rest of his life. On the other hand, after all they'd gone through, the discovery seemed somehow appropriate.

He decided he was in mild shock.

"Television," Sammy said. "I think it's the news. They're broadcasting on over a hundred channels. I can switch—"

"Wait!" Eric said.

The man had disappeared, being replaced by a brown crescent world, flecked with metallic dots, floating in space beside a huge sun. The planet rotated noticeably as they watched, the patterns of what must have been dust storms shifting constantly, and Eric realized they were seeing time-lapse photography, taken from a point in high orbit above the world. Then the sun began to swell and a hard lump tightened his throat. He told himself that it was ridiculous, that he didn't even know these people, that they weren't even *really* people, but it didn't help. A raging geyser of fusion-fueled whips slapped the brown surface and set it aflow in red rivers of hell. The planet's atmosphere elongated and stretched, as if it were at the mercy of a mad god's fanning, before being blown into space.

The view suddenly changed. They were now inside a dying city, probably underground, hopping from point to point along lengthy silver corridors toppling into ruin, beside green courtyards blackening and smoking. And everywhere there were people, running without a chance of escape, and falling into kicking balls of fire. . . .

"Turn it off!" Jeanie cried.

Sammy did so. The holograph went blank. Eric wished he could empty his mind as easily. His half-digested meal turned in his stomach. He looked at the nova and now saw the sharp edge of its beauty. It was a killer.

Eric had read in history tapes about natural calamities that had taken hundreds of thousands of lives: the outbreaks of the plague in Europe in the fifteenth and nineteenth centuries; the typhoons that had hit Bangladesh in the late twentieth century; the massive meteor that had vaporized the Titan community a hundred years ago. But the destruction of an entire civilization went beyond a tragedy. Eric was not given to religious references, but it seemed to him like some kind of galactic sin. And he couldn't help feeling guilty about it, though he did not know why.

"All those people are dead?" Cleo asked, stunned.

"All those on the planet must have died a few days ago," Strem said. "But from where are we receiving these transmissions?"

"Some must have escaped," Eric whispered.

Sammy nodded. "Yes. The stream of ions is the exhaust of a huge fleet heading away from the nova. Look at this."

The cube was suddenly jammed with a black circular plate of space pinpointed with countless minute craft trailing fine purple flares. Scale was impossible to judge. The ships appeared dangerously close together. Sammy addressed his unspoken concerns.

"Each of those ships is half a mile in diameter, separated from each other by a minimum of ten miles. What appears to be the flagship at the center—it is actually at the tip of a cone-shaped formation pointed at a neighboring star—is almost two miles in diameter. There are three hundred and eighty-two ships in the fleet."

"How far out are they?" Eric asked, his heartbeat in high gear.

"Approximately twice our distance from the nova. About five billion miles into deep space."

Eric frowned. "That can't be. They're using a primitive drive. . . . What's their speed?"

"You're really asking how long they've been under

way," Sammy said. "Based on their present velocity and rate of acceleration, assuming the Earth-size planet was their home world, which was undoubtedly the case—five years."

"Boy, they must be bored by now," Strem said, "cooped up for all that time."

Eric was impressed. Sammy's earlier comment about the surface of the world being incapable of supporting life for the last century had not been contradicted. Apparently these people had gone underground, and into orbit, where they hadn't simply cowered until the end. Probably using their world as a shield, staying in the planetary shadow, and ferrying materials into orbit from beneath the barren crust, they had constructed a flotilla larger than The Patrol's. A pity it had only a fraction of The Patrol's speed. Yet that is what amazed Eric, that they should have the guts to challenge interstellar space at a snail's pace.

"How far away is the nearest star?" he asked.

"For them," Sammy said, "centuries."

"And you say you haven't spotted any Patrol cruisers in the area?" he asked.

"None," Sammy replied.

"And the coolant's still contaminated?"

"Yes."

Eric studied the ships. With all those blazing rockets, the aliens would have to have coolant somewhere aboard. "This is a rear view. Are we behind the fleet?"

"Roughly," Sammy said.

Eric glanced at Strem, who held his eyes a long time before big smiles filled both their faces. "Can we change direction and intercept them?" Eric asked Sammy.

"We can alter our course toward them. For that, the drive would only have to be on for a moment. But to intercept them, we would have to kill almost our entire velocity. We'd heat up quick. We could explode."

"What are the chances of that happening?" Jeanie asked.

"Excellent," Sammy said.

"We've got to try it," Strem said. "We don't have any other choice."

"You said we had plenty of options." Jeanie said.

"I'm the captain," Strem replied. "I have to say things like that." He rubbed his palms together hungrily. "I knew something would turn up."

"Granted that we don't blow up decelerating," Eric said, "can we realistically board one of their ships, find coolant, and get back out without being spotted? We look different, we talk different, and we probably smell different."

"I've got wigs in my case!" Cleo exclaimed. "I can dye them white and style them any way we want. And I've got my stage makeup. It would be a cinch to paint ourselves gold."

"What about our eyes?" Eric asked.

"We could wear sunglasses," Strem said.

"We're talking about sneaking aboard an alien vessel," Eric said, "not going to the beach."

Cleo jumped to her feet. "Don't you guys remember my band's last show?" she cried impatiently. "We wore *fulleye* red contact lenses! They made us look like demons. I've got them with me. I can stain them green!"

"In a crisis such as this," Strem said, "it's always nice to have an extraterrestrial makeup artist handy."

"As far as their language is concerned," Sammy said, "we have a couple of points in our favor. Before I told you guys about the transmissions, I flipped through a few of their channels and I noticed several languages being spoken. The planet must have still been divided into countries when the nova started up. If we entered a ship, it might not be that unusual that we could not speak the local dialect. Also, I can set *Excalibur*'s computers to decipher the languages. Whoever goes aboard could have a microtranslator implanted in one ear. Whatever was said would be immediately changed into English. This implant could also double as a communicator tied back to *Excalibur*. I'm right, Strem, in assuming your uncle has translators aboard?"

Strem nodded. "With all the different types of people in The Union with whom a trader has to do business, a trader can't get by without them. So many worlds have developed their own slang."

Eric was beginning to feel a mildly intoxicating combination of unreality and excitement. They were going to try it—the graviton drive permitting; they couldn't just glide forever into nothing. "There is an alternative we're not considering," he said slowly.

"Yeah," Jeanie said. "Why don't we just ask them for some coolant?"

Strem and Cleo laughed. Sammy looked worried. Eric was surprised that it was Sammy who initiated the argument against the idea.

"We can't do that," he said seriously. "They would want to know who we were, where we came from, *how* we got here, and how *Excalibur* works. Their propulsion systems are clearly far behind our own. We don't have the authority or the right to tamper with an alien culture."

"Damn right," Strem said. "Sorry, Jeanie, but if they got hold of the graviton and hyper drives, they could make trouble for The Union."

"They could even shoot at us and damage us and take *Excalibur*," Cleo put in.

"Why are you all assuming they're hostile?" Jeanie asked, irritated. "They're such good-looking people."

"They're also a desperate people." Strem snorted. "Imagine, trying to get to the stars in those clunkers."

Clearly Strem had a different appreciation of the aliens' efforts, Eric thought. He held his tongue. He didn't know these beings, other than their beautiful voices. He didn't want to take the responsibility of handing over advanced technology. Besides, if he pushed the issue, the others, except for Jeanie, would just vote him down. There was no reason to take up a losing cause. At least, not right now, anyway.

6

The hours of anticipation had passed. The plan was to approach across the charged wake created by the hundreds of ion drives. The turbulence would play havoc with their own failing power, but Sammy felt it offered the best cover from watchful eyes. They also hoped their speed, slow next to a Patrol cruiser but stupendous compared to the fleet, would catch the aliens unaware. It was their intention to sneak in beside a ship along the perimeter of the formation and look for an air lock that wasn't locked.

They'd been watching a lot of television. The *Kaulikans*—as they referred to themselves—were still an enigma, but Eric had not expected to absorb the soul of an alien culture in a few hours. More and more, he was afraid that if they did get aboard a ship, they'd be spotted by the first person they said hello to (which was, by the way, *boo* in the Kaulikans' predominant language). Outside work situations the Kaulikans used a multitude of hand gestures to communicate, many quick and intricate; these were not something that could be mastered in a crash course. Thank heavens the aliens had a standard issue of five fingers.

Flipping through the channels, several other social characteristics had struck Eric. The Kaulikans were great lovers of romantic operas—they were *all* exquisite sopranos—specifically, a type where the people in the audience danced while the performers on stage sang. They also appeared a nonviolent race; he hadn't found a program where one Kaulikan had hit another Kaulikan. Of course, Strem said, it was probably a social taboo to get mad, but they being Earth people and alien to this culture would still have to stay on their guard.

The aliens smiled when they were happy, nodded when they meant yes and shook their heads when they meant no. Although the coincidence raised interesting philosophical implications on the nature of intelligent life everywhere in the universe, they didn't dwell on them.

Eric and Strem were to be the only ones to enter the ship. Cleo threw a fit at being counted out, but Eric suspected it was more of an act; Sammy was able to pacify her easily. Jeanie wanted no part of the adventure, and it was decided by vote that Sammy was too valuable, with his technical knowledge, to risk. Sammy took the decision quietly, though his disappointment was obvious. The main reason the exploration belonged to Eric and Strem, though, was because they were physically the strongest; they were hoping to come away with twenty gallons of coolant each, and the stuff was heavy. At least along the outer rims of the alien vessels.

The Kaulikans generated their gravity the old-fashioned way—they rotated. On the route in, the two of them were going to carry inflatable containers under their jackets. The return trip, with the bulbous bottles on their backs, was planned to be quick and smooth, and without too many questions.

On the other hand, the question of who was best qualified was meaningless. Eric and Strem were going because they wanted to go, and no one was going to stop them.

The fleet was getting closer, visible out the forward window as a nebulous cloud, approximately twenty million miles distant. Eric studied the holographic image, magnified and adjusted for the Doppler effect, instead of relying upon his naked eye. The craft were all of essentially the same design: three massive silver wheels spaced equally along a gray central shaft that ended in the rear in a huddle of four black domes. On the surface, these domes appeared to generate the purple fountains of charged particles that drove the Kaulikans toward the stars. The flagship at the tip of the fleet was an exception; it had nine wheels and was entirely blue.

"This stuff smells," Strem complained as Jeanie rubbed her closed-eye boyfriend's face with golden oil. Eric had already been oiled and had been pleased to see it was an improvement. He looked like a well-tanned tourist who had just returned from a month on an exotic beach in the center of a globular cluster. The white of his painted eyebrows and eyelashes didn't look that bad either, though he had yet to try on the curly wig as the white dye on it was still drying.

"Hush, don't move," Jeanie said. "The smell goes away when it dries."

"Then it starts to itch," Eric muttered.

"Two minutes," Sammy said. "Start tidying up our loose ends."

"These lenses are going to look wicked on you guys!" Cleo said, sitting squat on the floor, coloring the contacts. Eric knelt beside her and began collecting pieces of clothing, scissors, tape, brushes—putting them back in Cleo's suitcase.

"Have you decided where to attach *Excalibur*?" he asked Sammy.

"Yes." Besides navigating the ship, Sammy was studying a perimeter Kaulikan craft on a screen under extreme magnification. "We are going to tuck in the rear wheel. There is a lip along the edge where we should be able to hide."

"Be sure to put us down with our heads toward the axis," Eric said. As soon as they were locked onto the rotating structure, they would be under the influence of the Kaulikans' pseudogravity, and would hit the ceiling if they didn't orient themselves properly. Sammy knew that, of course.

"Enough!" Jeanie told Strem, putting down her oilcloth. She laughed. "You look so cute!"

Strem opened his eyes and immediately strode to his sleeping quarters and a mirror, reappearing a minute later. "Not bad, not bad, probably wouldn't even get me expelled from school. Where's that jacket I'm supposed to wear?"

The opants, when turned off, resembled the plain clothes the average Kaulikan appeared to wear while on duty. Yet, Eric was as much concerned about the flaws in their dress as the discrepancies in their voices and skin color. "Resembled" and "identical" were two words with plenty of room in between where suspicions could be raised. What were they going to say if they got caught? Well, you see Mr. Kaulikan, we really did have green eyes but they changed color when we stared at the nova too long. . . .

"Say, 'I'm from one of the farm worlds,' " Eric told Strem. To the aliens, their ships were worlds. As they had to spend the rest of their lives inside them, it was easy to understand why.

Strem glanced out the window at the purple nebula, which was steadily resolving into tiny individual candle-lights. "*Les kau tee mick.*"

"No, that's 'I really must be on my way.' "

"It doesn't matter, Sammy can tell me what to say. Hey, why don't we just learn the line: 'I'm deaf, thank you, good-bye.' "

"Because then someone would want to take us to one of their doctors," Eric said, putting the last of Cleo's paraphernalia away. "Finished with our eyes?" he asked her.

Cleo held two of the green contacts up to the light. "Perfect."

"Buckle down, everybody," Sammy said. "Time to put on the brakes."

Sammy wisely did not add: *And see if we don't kill ourselves.*

Eric suspected neither of the girls fully realized how dangerous the deceleration would be; they had been far more tense before Jeret's customs check.

Eric stowed Cleo's case and took a seat between Strem and Sammy, fastening a crisscrossed elastic belt over his chest. He glanced at Strem and received a golden thumbs up—Jeanie had also oiled their hands—and it seemed somehow extra lucky.

Sammy rolled *Excalibur* until the ship's nose was pointed toward the nova, then activated the graviton drive. Besides slowing them drastically, the drive would also, theoretically, repel the energy of the Kaulikans' wide ion train. As the low hum began to shake the ship, changing swiftly into the brief high-pitched whine, Eric noticed nothing different than during their accelera-tion out of Earth orbit. A glance at the control console, however, revealed several additional indicators creeping into the danger zone.

They were now approximately twice the orbit of Pluto from the nova and were able to look at it through unfiltered windows. With the added distance, the layers of expelled gas appeared denser, and it was pleasant to imagine they were watching the cooling birth of a super being's central planet, and not the remains of a mortal's dead solar system. How often, Eric wondered, were the eyes of the remaining Kaulikans drawn to their own windows, to see what had driven them from home?

Suddenly, a red haze began to blur the nova as a deep but soft drone filled the cabin. Eric did not know if the haze and noise was due to the overloading graviton drive or the impact of the changed particles on the ship's force field. He hesitated to ask Sammy, who was, to put it mildly, very busy, staring without blinking at the information being fed to him by *Excalibur*'s computers, his two hands instinctively adjusting the controls.

Eric was surprised at himself. He was afraid, but the emotion seemed somehow removed from him perhaps because, if the end came, he would not have a chance to know it. The drone reminded him of the sound of water flushing the hull of a plowing minisub, and he thought of the evening he had chased sharks with Strem in the warm sea off Baja, only hours after hearing of Strem's wild vacation plans. It seemed as though it were years ago.

"How are we doing?" Strem asked quickly.

"If I can answer that question in a moment," Sammy said, "we're doing very well indeed."

A nerve-taunting bell went off, and Cleo and Jeanie let out a cry. Sammy quieted it with the flip of a switch. They were committed. The drone thickened and got louder, becoming harsher, sounding more like the thun-

der of an approaching storm on an open prairie. The
red haze changed to a yellow glare, hurting their eyes.
Sammy lowered the shields, but the enforced blindness
was dubious comfort. Eric's chair began to shake violently, and he could feel the vertebrae in his spine
rattling. He took a deep breath and didn't bother to let
it go.

"Is the drive overheating?" Strem shouted over the
roar.

"No!" Sammy shouted back. "It's melting!"

Eric heard the crack of sparks and smelled ozone. He
wondered for a moment, if it were to end now, what he
would miss the most.

There was a horrendous bump, followed by two more
murderous blows. They could have been ramming walls
of stone. Then the bottom seemed to drop out of
Excalibur; the computer had automatically given up
maintaining the ship's gravity, no doubt trying to pre-
serve every last morsel of energy.

A tornado swept Eric's sense of balance, and he felt
nauseous. The white wig he was supposed to wear
swiped the side of his head. Another bell began to yell,
and this time Sammy was unable to reach the switch to
turn it off. The thunder swelled to the roar of a volcano.
Eric tasted blood in his mouth. He had bitten his
tongue, or his lip, or both.

The lights went out. Someone screamed.

Then there was nothing. No movement, no sound.
Nothing.

The lights came back on.

Eric looked at his friends. They looked at him. Naturally, Strem was the first one to relocate his mouth. His

words came out as muffled whispers. Their eardrums were throbbing.

"So I guess we're alive," he said.

Eric smiled and nodded and felt his neck crack. Cleo's suitcase floated by his head. They were in free fall, and a part of him wanted to fly. Smoke wafted from a minor electrical discharge in the ceiling. The control console was a blanket of red lights. It did not matter. Strem's guess was right.

Sammy lifted the shields from the windows. All sense of perspective turned inside out. A long curving silver wall now hung above *Excalibur*, which his intellect could only tenuously connect with the tiny objects he had been studying in the holographic cube minutes before. This was the edge of one of the Kaulikans' ships' three rotating wheels. A sparkling purple jet fanned out behind them and he felt its warmth in his chest.

"They're really here," Jeanie whispered in awe.

Sammy took a quick inspection of the Kaulikan ship and began to turn *Excalibur* on her tail. The colossal wheel floated closer. Its white hull was virtually seamless, and Eric wondered if entry would be as easy as it had sounded from millions of miles away. He did spot, however, a small antenna dish—which in all probability was bigger than their own ship—and watched as it drifted along a sweeping arc as the wheel spun. Then the antenna appeared to halt as Sammy synchronized their drift with that of the huge hub. They glided inwards toward a shadow cast by the curled rim of the bright metal walls.

"Think they know we're here?" Strem breathed.

"Your guess is as good as mine," Sammy replied. Then he abruptly leaned forward, repeatedly pressing a single button.

"What is it?" Eric asked.

"One second," Sammy said.

The curve of the wheel's rim opened into a dim hollow. *Excalibur* had been constructed in space and was not designed to land. Technically, this was a docking and not a landing, but as they were going under the influence of external gravity, it would have been nice to have shock pads. If they didn't touch down gently, the bang would reverberate throughout the Kaulikan craft.

"We have a problem," Sammy said finally. "Our dampers are fused in place."

"Does that mean we can't keep the drive on?" Strem asked.

"It means we can't turn it off," Sammy said. "Not and restart it. I can idle the graviton flux and hold us in place but we'll just keep heating."

"For how long?" Cleo asked.

"Until we blow up," Sammy said.

"How much time do we have?" Eric asked.

"If we can keep a minimum idle," Sammy said, "maybe six hours, maybe less. I was really hoping to turn most of our systems off."

Eric hardly felt the touchdown on the inside rim of the rotating wheel. The hovering wigs and clothes settled to the floor. Looking straight up, through a gape cut by the shadowed rim and the reflecting hull, he saw a dozen nearby Kaulikan ships, much more widely spaced than he could have imagined from his earlier examination of the fleet. *Excalibur* was only a needle in a spread-out haystack, and it gave him reason to hope they had not been spotted.

They undid their belts, stood and stretched—even Sammy, who they had been beginning to believe had grown into his seat. Their relief at having survived the deceleration was cooled by the new deadline the fused damper had given them. Plus, there was the not so minor consideration, at least from Eric's side, that within minutes they would be coming face-to-face with aliens. He was anxious to get going.

"I didn't see any air locks when we were coming down," Strem said, squeezing one of the drying white hairpieces over his head, ignoring Cleo's and Jeanie's snickers.

Sammy pointed out the window at the dark artificial valley in which *Excalibur* was nestled. "From sensor readings, there appear to be several placed along this rim. Walk in either direction long enough and you will come to one."

"Should be interesting trying to open it," Eric said. He pulled on his opant coat and glanced down at his gray slippers, realizing none of them had thought to note what type of shoes the Kaulikans wore. It was too late to worry about it now.

"We'll bring lasers," Strem said. "We can always cut it."

"No." Eric shook his head. "Absolutely not."

"You could set off an alarm that way," Sammy agreed. "There will be a remote eye on your pressure suits and opant belts. When you get to an air lock, I'll be able to study it with you, and we'll figure something out."

"I'm bringing a laser, anyway," Strem said. "I'm not going in there unarmed."

Eric was annoyed. "And do what with it? If we get caught, we can't fight our way back to *Excalibur*."

"Why not?" Strem asked.

"You could just stun them," Cleo said. "You wouldn't have to kill anybody."

"Listen to yourselves," Eric said. "Here we're about to make the most incredible contact and you're talking about confrontations. Can't you see, if we get caught we can't give these people the impression we're a hostile race?"

"Suit yourself," Strem said. "I'm bringing a gun. I'll hide it under my coat, and no one will know I have it. I won't use it unless I'm forced to."

"If we *do* get caught," Eric said as patiently as he could, "the fact that you have a weapon will be bad enough. It won't matter if you use it or not. Remember, we are the ones who are trespassing."

Strem looked puzzled. "Why is it that at times like this, you always start worrying about the implications of every blessed thing we're going to do?"

"For the life of me," Eric grumbled, "I can't remember another time like this."

"I agree with Strem," Cleo said.

"I agree with Eric," Jeanie said.

Sammy, true to his uninvolved nature, didn't vote either way. In the end, Strem took a gun from the weapons cabinet, but before he tucked it away, Eric made sure it was locked in the stun position.

Sammy fitted the implants in their ears, and they turned on a Kaulikan TV program to give themselves a trial run. They quickly discovered that when an alien was speaking, they had to consciously block out what was being said in order to catch the whispered mechanical voice in their heads. The translation, however, was the easy part. Though remaining on the bridge, Sammy would be able, by virtue of the implants, to hear everything that was said. They had previously decided that when he'd received a Kaulikan's spoken words, and had had them translated, he would give an appropriate response in *English* to the ship's computer which would then relay it to them in Basic Kaulikan. It sounded good in theory but when they tried simulating an anticipated conversation, they decided they would be lucky if they were mistaken for stuttering morons.

The contacts were uncomfortable and hard to see through. Cleo defended herself by saying she had had to use several layers of the green dye to get the proper shade. *Blind* stuttering morons.

There was no sense in waiting. Cleo blow-dried their wigs, and Jeanie touched up their face color. They climbed into their pressure suits and headed for *Excalibur's* air lock. Eric very much enjoyed the girls' good-bye kisses, especially Jeanie's tearful, "Come back soon." He was beginning to feel scared, but it was the kind of scared that made him feel extraordinarily alive. They slipped their inflatable containers through the collars of the opant coats and donned their helmets. Sammy shook their gloved hands.

"Be careful," he said.

Of course, it was too late for advice like that.

7

The first thing Eric did when he stepped outside was turn on his helmet lamp. The light came out green on a green metallic ground. With the contacts he was going to miss out on whatever colors the Kaulikan universe had to offer.

He moved straight out of the air lock toward the nearest wall and looked "up" toward the end of the gray central shaft and the black domes that encircled the shimmering ionic trail. What the alien technology lacked in sophistication, it made up for in magnitude. He stood, unable to stop staring, until he started to feel dizzy and had to put a hand out to steady himself. The rotation of the wheel was disorienting.

"Are you okay?" Strem asked, putting his hand on his shoulder, shining his helmet lamp directly in his eyes.

"Yes." Eric straightened. *Excalibur* blocked one side of the dark tunnel formed by the rim of the spinning wheel, a silent black cylinder whose outline could be seen only as a silhouette against the star field. But the other direction curved upwards without obstruction toward an inverted horizon that would bring them back to where they had started if they followed it long enough. Eric pointed to the Kaulikans' glowing purple tail, which seemed to disappear into infinity. "Quite a view, huh?" he said.

"I've got to admit, it is," Strem said. "I just can't understand how they could work so long building these ships and not invent the graviton or hyper drives. They mustn't be as intelligent as we are."

"If I remember correctly, Dr. Pernel discovered the principles of the graviton flux entirely by accident, which led to the discovery of hyper relays. We were lucky; they weren't."

"Ah, maybe."

They started away from *Excalibur*, plodding under the weight of their pressure suits, which had been designed for free fall. Eric estimated their gravity at eighty percent Earth's. The side force or acceleration generated by the Kaulikan drive was barely noticeable. Then again, he wouldn't have been surprised to learn that their drive had been on continuously for the last five years.

The first part of their slow walk was uneventful. The hull floor was flat, devoid of equipment. Eric repeatedly found his eyes drawn to the central shaft, soundlessly spinning its massive plates on what must have been the largest ball bearings in this quadrant of the galaxy. He suspected that was where engineering would be located, which was where they'd probably find their forty gallons of ethylene glycol.

Two-hundred yards from *Excalibur* they came to a circular hatch on the ground with a light in the center and a handle at either end. There were no buttons to push, no knobs to spin. They stared at it for awhile before Sammy came over the line.

("Pull on it. Turn it. Play with it. Open it.")

They tried to turn it clockwise and counterclockwise, but it didn't budge. Yanking on the handles didn't help matters. Eric thought it would be fitting to travel hundreds of light years, survive a nova and a mad deceleration, and then not be able to get past the door. Finally, frustrated, Strem kicked the light, and lo and behold, that worked. The hatch eased up a couple of inches and they were able to turn it a half revolution clockwise until it stopped and swung open. They peeked inside. It was awfully dark.

"Who wants to go first?" Strem said.

"Who was the first man to step on the moon?" Eric asked.

"Armstrong."

"You see, you remember. I'm going first." Eric knelt by the hole, found a ladder in his light, turned around, and gingerly stuck his right foot inside, letting his heel come to rest on a firm flat rung. That wasn't so bad. He put his left foot on the next rung, counting ten steps as he carefully descended. From the spacing of the rungs and the height of a closed door at one end of the cramped air lock, he estimated that the Kaulikans must be about as tall as themselves; another one of a dozen particulars he had been worried about.

Eric waved for Strem to come down and peered through a circular window in the door, glimpsing a lit corridor at the end of a brief dark hallway. He watched for a couple of minutes; no one walked by.

"Want me to kick them?" Strem asked a moment later as the two of them bent over the row of three differently shaded green lights adjacent to the door. Checking to be sure Strem had closed the hatch behind him, Eric put his hand over the top light. Nothing happened. He tried the second one and got the same result. With the third time, though, the walls began to glow as atmosphere rushed into the cubicle. They turned off their head lamps, and Strem went to remove his helmet. Eric stopped him.

"Organism check," Eric said, reaching into his suit pouch and removing a white spongy cube sealed in clear plastic. He tore off the wrapper. If the sponge turned black within a minute, there was probably something fatal in the air.

"I hope we don't catch anything from them," Strem said, watching.

"I hope we don't give them anything."

"There you go again. We've had the Union Shot Series. We can't infect anybody on any planet."

"We can't infect anybody that's human. We may not be doing these people a favor by dropping in this way."

The cube remained white. Eric put it back in his pouch and they pulled off their helmets.

The air was warm, slightly humid, and smelled like honey. Eric had half expected stale recycled odors. He took a long deep breath, tasting a high oxygen content.

A light now shone in the center of the door. They pressed it and the door opened. The short hallway outside the air lock was a locker room, and they were able to stow their pressure suits in two empty cabinets. Eric scowled as Strem removed his gun from a clasp on his oxygen tank and hid it inside his opant jacket. Strem just shook his head, muttering under his breath about moralistic obsessions.

"Sammy, how's your reception?" Eric asked. He was scarcely aware of the implant inside his ear. The remote eye was a pinpoint dot at the center of their belts.

("Audio and video are both excellent. Now get away from the air lock as quickly as you can.")

The corridor outside the second door was empty, stretching beyond its upside-down horizon to the left, but dead-ending in what appeared to be an elevator on the right. The featureless ceiling was low, another foot and it would have touched Strem's fluffy white head, and the floor was an undistinguished carpet. The walls, on the other hand, were decorated with abstract mosaics—at least they looked abstract to Eric—made up of countless tiny rock tiles. He was sorely tempted to slip out his contacts and see if the artwork didn't take on definition with the help of a color besides green. Nevertheless, despite the limitations of his vision, the designs appealed to him. They seemed somehow optimistic.

They entered the elevator at the end of the corridor. The single door closed behind them. This time there were six lights to choose from, each underlined with an imprinted symbol.

"Sammy, what are these markings?" Eric asked.

("The numerals one through six, counting from the top.")

"There has got to be more floors in this wheel than six," Eric said thoughtfully. "We'll probably have to find another elevator. Sammy, I'm for heading for the axis. How does that sound?"

("I was thinking the same thing. That's where their power supply will be. I can track you in case you start going in circles.")

Eric looked at Strem, who was fidgeting noticeably. "What's wrong?" he asked.

"Nothing."

"Are you scared?"

"No!"

"Don't be afraid to admit it. Just because I'm not doesn't mean you don't have to be."

Strem touched the bottom light. They jerked upward. "I'm fine, I just have to go to the bathroom."

A line of light shone through the translucent panels to the sides of the elevator door, then a second line, as they passed through the levels. Eric detected no noticeable lessening of gravity. "Why didn't you go to the bathroom before we left?" he asked.

"I forgot."

"You didn't forget your gun." Eric added, "We can't go back."

"I didn't say we should."

"You'll just have to hold it."

Strem swallowed. "Maybe we can find a bathroom while we're looking around. They've got to have bathrooms."

"Strem, we're in an alien ship full of aliens. We have only so many hours to find coolant and get out of here before our own ship explodes. We can't go looking for bathrooms."

"If it were you, Eric, you'd feel a lot differently."

"I doubt you could even figure out how to use their toilets."

"But if they . . ." Strem didn't get a chance to finish. As they went to pass through the third level, the elevator halted, and the door swished open. Standing outside were two Kaulikan men.

They were shorter than Eric and Strem, and thinner, dressed in the plain long-sleeve shirts and double-front-pocketed pants Eric had noted on their TV programs. Even through the hazy contacts, their faces looked smooth and their eyes bright. Eric caught himself staring, but it was not so much at their difference from himself as at their similarity. Why, these were people, *real* people. They smiled faintly, stepping into the elevator. "*Boo*," they said softly.

"*Boo*," Eric said automatically, tugging on Strem's elbow, pulling him forward.

"*Boe*," Strem coughed out, stumbling from the elevator. The door closed at their backs and they were alone in another empty corridor. They stood for a moment with their breath held, then burst out laughing. Nothing was really funny; all the tension they'd accumulated since leaving Earth just seemed to pour out in that moment.

"*Boe*." Eric chuckled, leaning against a wall.

"*Boo, boe*, what the hell," Strem said, catching his breath. "What now?"

Eric touched the light at the side of the elevator. "Let's wait for it to come back."

The cubicle, thankfully empty, did so a moment later. They got in and went up to level six. This time Eric noticed a slight decrease in his weight, perhaps three pounds. If they were to reach weightlessness by the time they got to the axis, the wheel would have to have about fifty levels.

The elevator opened onto a wide hallway overflowing with curly-haired Kaulikans all heading in one direction. Chimes sang through the air. Eric smelled food.

"Well?" Strem said.

"This elevator can't take us any further," Eric whispered. "Let's join the flow."

The crowd was not as intimidating as he would have imagined; the numbers made it easier to blend in. The Kaulikans kept a brisk pace. Maybe they only ate once a day and were hungry. Eric and Strem hugged the wall as the hallway curved toward what was unmistakably the cafeteria.

They were the tallest ones there, but not exceptionally so. The background chatter was much less than it would have been on Earth in a similar setting. The quiet blend of the melodious voices, male and female, was pleasant to the ear. Eric tugged on his right earlobe, activating his translator. As the high-gain mike automatically picked up the loudest word being spoken at any instant, he was bombarded with pieces of conversations.

"*Rak knew what was best . . . She wept a short while . . . Yeast pods need enrichment . . . Nova's eye . . . Core might rupture . . . We danced by the waterfall in the twilight . . . Busy the next twenty cycles . . . First Councillor's broadcast was inspiring . . . I am forgetting already . . . I never will . . .*"

Strem was poking his side. Eric turned off the translator. "We're going to lunch!" Strem hissed.

"Aren't you hungry?"

"No! Let's turn around!"

"Not against this crowd. There may be a bathroom in the cafeteria. Sammy, what is it called?"

("*Toto.* Just make sure the stalls are separate. We don't want Strem taking his pants down in front of anybody.")

"Very funny," Strem said, fuming.

Some things would probably be the same in another dimension. Kaulikan custom dictated that they first pick up a food tray. The material felt like plastic and probably was. There were bowls and spoons, but no knives or forks. Eric quickly saw why the latter was unnecessary. The crowd split into two lines in front of two rows of automatic food dispensers. One put the bowl in, and the machine gave out a serving. None of the food looked as though it needed to be cut: mushes of grains and tiny pieces of fruits or vegetables or *something* that appeared to have been grown. No one was taking seconds and, glancing around, he realized none of the aliens were overweight. Strangely enough, he began to feel hungry. He stuck in one of his bowls and got back something that resembled rice. A pity it had to be green. Strem followed his example, collecting a serving of what could have been Jell-O. They started down the line. Eric reactivated his translator.

Halfway through the dispensers, his four bowls almost full, Eric made his first genuine alien contact. She was approximately his age—assuming the Kaulikans had a similar life span—and had a sling around her right arm. Balancing her tray in her good hand, she was unknowingly bumped by another Kaulikan and lost one of her bowls over her uniform. Eric set down his tray and stooped to help her. The gesture was spontaneous, begun before he realized the risk he was running. He picked up her bowl and helped her resteady her tray. Only when he was through with his good deed did he look her straight in the face. She was beautiful.

She smiled. "*Kanee.*"

"*Thank you, brother,*" the translator whispered in its neutral voice. Eric waited for Sammy and *Excalibur*'s computers to provide him with a reasonable response. And he waited. Finally, "*Schelle.*"

"*Schelle,*" he said, turning away, but not before he saw her expression change to something he assumed indicated puzzlement: a slight pinch of her lips and a sudden backward tilt of her head. He pressed forward, not looking back.

The cafeteria sitting-area was an arena. Hundreds of tables and thousands of chairs fanned out from a tall central fountain embedded with a crystalline sculpture resembling a huge snowflake. The sculpture was slowly spinning beneath the cascade of waters and the glitter of dozens of narrow beams of light projected from the intricate mosaic ceiling. People were gathering around the fountain, and for that reason Eric steered away from it, choosing a spot somewhere in between the furthest corner and the thickest part of the crowd.

"I'd like to know *what* we are doing here?" Strem demanded, sitting across from him. "You didn't have time to search for a bathroom, and now you're having lunch!"

Eric tried his "rice." The sensitivity of the cube he had employed in the air lock—to even stray food odors—was such that it was unlikely there was anything harmful in the dish. The rice tasted like marshmallows. "The elevator couldn't lead us any closer to the central shaft. We couldn't just stand there. And you weren't exactly bursting over with ideas."

"Well, I have a fantastic idea now. Let's get the hell out of here."

"But, I'm hungry."

"Eric, damnit, what was all that about being aboard an alien ship full of aliens?"

"Sammy, how's the Preeze Cap keeping?"

("I wouldn't go back for dessert, but we're not going to explode this minute.")

"We need time to orient ourselves," Eric told Strem. "Learn from what we've seen."

But that was only part of it, at least as far as he was concerned. When he had entered the cafeteria line, the pressure to be about their mission had suddenly and inexplicably lessened for him. Now he felt an eagerness to look around, to go exploring and soak up the culture. He wondered where the girl with the sore arm was sitting.

"How many would you say this cafeteria serves?" Eric asked.

"About ten thousand."

"I bet they have one of these halls in each wheel. They probably use them in shifts to economize on space. If we take ten thousand times three—for the number of wheels—times three again—for the numbers of shifts—we've got almost a hundred thousand Kaulikans."

"So?"

"With that many people, they've got to have a lot of bathrooms."

"Would you shut up about that."

"Don't you see? No one could get to know that many people in five years. Chances are we won't be spotted just because we're a new face in town."

Strem nodded. "That's good to know." He leaned closer. "I liked that girl you bumped into. Great body."

"Speaking of whom . . ." He found her, and had to wonder if she weren't following them. She was sitting only a few tables away, off to the right in the direction of the fountain, eating alone and facing their way. She noticed his attention and smiled. He quickly averted his eyes. "Yours truly is sitting behind you," Eric muttered. "No, don't turn around. I think she caught my strange accent."

"More the reason to get out of here."

"We just got here. It might look funny if we leave immediately."

Eric noticed, however, how swiftly everyone was eating. Keeping afloat in this void probably took everyone's best effort; the Kaulikans wouldn't have the luxury of wasting time. "Eat your food," he said.

Strem sampled his salad. "These things taste like candy." Strem tried something that resembled mashed potatoes. "And this tastes as though it's melting ice cream. No wonder it's taking these people so long to get to the stars; they're all sugar addicts."

"You know," Eric said, "we might be going about this

all wrong. Here we are stumbling around trying to avoid contact. Maybe we should be doing the opposite— maybe we should go up to someone, introduce ourselves as visitors from another ship with a language problem, and ask to be shown around."

Strem snickered. "Does "Green Eyes" have anything to do with this change in strategy?"

"All the girls here have green eyes."

Strem was not fooled. "*Who* should we ask to show us around?"

Eric shrugged. "Green Eyes. Look, she appears to be about our age. I doubt she's into reporting things to the authorities, teenagers usually aren't. Plus, we've already made contact." He added, "I think she likes me."

"What makes you think that?"

"My optimistic nature."

"I don't know. It's risky."

"Our being here is risky."

Strem lowered his voice. "Could you ask her where the *toto* is?"

Eric nodded, standing. "Wish me luck. Sammy, get ready."

("This should be interesting.")

Eric wanted to introduce himself quickly before he had a chance to chicken out. On Earth, at parties and dances, he'd always had a hard time crossing the room and starting a conversation with a strange girl. But this girl was *so* strange, it seemed to make it easier—until Eric began to realize that in all their preparation, they hadn't given themselves Kaulikan names. He didn't even know if the Kaulikans had last names, or numbers. And why did he leave his ship to come to hers? Did these people take vacations?

She was concentrating on her food and didn't notice

Eric's approach. He stood to her left, slightly behind her, thinking that he'd never met a girl on Earth that could rival her, feeling his confidence and doubts swinging up and down.

Her hair was longer than the majority of her people's, more wavy than curly, reaching almost to her waist. Her face somehow managed to convey both mystery and innocence: her mouth was wide, full-lipped, alluring, while her cheeks had a youth's roundness, perfectly complementing her button nose.

(*"Boo."*)

"I know, Sammy," Eric muttered.

The girl turned. Her eyes were big and round. She set down her spoon and gracefully faced her left palm toward him and then toward herself.

(*"She is welcoming you."*)

Eric nodded and sat down. "*See mino toe fruz,*" he said quickly, pitching his voice high. (*I'm from one of the farm worlds.*) "*Se trez hoe Kaulikan tau, tire Kutz.*" (*I understand Kaulikan Basic, but speak it poorly.*)

These were two lines he had down pat. Nevertheless, his accent caused her to display the same puzzlement she'd had in the food line. She answered, and he had to strain to block out her words and concentrate on the translation. Her voice seemed to tickle the inside of his brain, silky and penetrating.

"*What language do you speak?*" The sterile translation asked. Eric waited for Sammy's response.

(*"Mea fie excelr."*)

"*Mea fie excelr,*" he said. What did that mean? Boy, this was complicated. And now she was answering in sign language!

(*"Say: 'Se Lutz' Hardly anyone in this fleet seems to know Lutz."*)

"*Se Lutz,*" Eric said.

She appeared satisfied. Apparently Lutzers were known for being weird. Her next remark had a lot of spunk in it.

"I've never met someone from off world. But I knew you were strangers. I am Vani."

Eric pointed to himself, hesitated. *"See Eric."*

"Eric," Vani murmured. *"Are you enjoying your visit?"*

He nodded.

"I am glad. Is your world much different than ours?"

He nodded.

"Thank you for helping me in line."

He nodded, wondering how much longer he could keep doing that. Sammy understood his predicament.

("Let's take a chance. English might not sound that much different than Lutz to her. Mutter to yourself how you want to respond, a phrase or two, as though you're trying to remember the Kaulikan Basic, and I will set your translator to immediately give you the corresponding words.")

Are you busy this Friday evening, he thought, scratching his forehead for a moment before realizing he might scratch away some of his gold stain. Despite the difficulties in the interaction, he was actually beginning to enjoy himself. But there was no sense beating around the bush.

"We are lost," he whispered to himself. *"Seei tie wohl."* "Could you please show us around?" *"Dohl heht?"* Was that it? He repeated the Kaulikan phrases to her. Her big eyes appeared to widen and she nodded.

"Because of my arm injury I have free time before study period. Would you like to see our farms and our garden?"

"Yes." *"Ki."* *"Ki,"* he repeated. She peered at him.

"Are your eyes all right?"

He looked away, back the way he had come. Strem

was watching. "Fumes." "*Zeowt*." He gestured to his eyes. "*Zeowt*," he said.

She was concerned, the doll. "*Are they healing quickly?*"

He nodded and stood suddenly, pointing to Strem, indicating he had to go get his friend. That was fine with Vani. He hurried away, pleased with his success and amazed at how easy it was to get on friendly terms with people in this place.

"Well?" Strem said impatiently, having finished the last of his candy salad.

"There are no bathrooms in this entire ship."

Strem would have looked green without the contacts. "But that's impossible. What do they do when? . . . How do they? . . . You're pulling my leg!"

Eric laughed. "I'm sure she can show you where the *toto* is. She has some free time to play guide. By the way, we're Lutzers."

"Who are they?"

"Beats me."

"Did you ask her to take us to engineering?"

"Not yet. She wants to show us her farms."

"I don't want to see her stupid farms."

Eric did; he was suddenly curious about every facet of these people's lives. "We need to build up some sort of rapport with her before we ask about the coolant."

"We may just build up suspicion. I say we go for broke, ask her where we can get the ethylene glycol."

"She'll ask what we want it for."

"Tell her we'll show her. Then when she gets it for us we can lead her back to the air lock and stun her and be on our merry way."

"You're not going to stun Vani!"

"*Vani?*" Strem laughed. "Hey, it won't hurt her. And when she wakes up, she'll have a great mystery to gossip about. What's the matter with you, Eric? You can't be falling for this girl. She isn't even a girl. I bet she doesn't even know how to kiss."

"I am not falling for her," Eric said coolly. "Sammy, what do you think?"

("Cleo and Jeanie . . .")

("Get her alone and give her a kiss," Cleo said. "I want to see what she does.")

("She strikes me as the take-it-slow type," Jeanie said. "I don't think you should kiss her or stun her on the first date.")

"I think you will feel less pressure once you visit the *toto*," Eric told Strem. It bothered him slightly that his whole encounter with Vani had been monitored by the others.

"You're not the only one who can talk to her," Strem said.

"Yes, I am. I told her you were deaf."

"What?"

"That's what you said to do earlier."

"I was only joking!"

"So am I. Come on, it's no big deal. She'll show us her farms for a few minutes, and then we'll steer her toward engineering."

Strem didn't say anything, but Eric couldn't help noticing how his hand strayed to the bulge under his jacket where his gun was hidden.

8

Vani was waiting patiently for them. Eric noticed she had eaten less than half her food. She said she had not been feeling very hungry the last few cycles. They dumped their trays at the edge of the cafeteria in what resembled an old-fashioned water well, and walked toward the exit. While leaving Strem put an elbow in Eric's ribs.

"Toto," Eric said, searching about. Vani understood immediately, pointing to two doors not far from where they had deposited their trays. Strem took off at a brisk walk.

"Your friend is big," Vani said.

Eric nodded. "Strem."

"Strem, Eric," Vani said to herself. *"Where on Kashi were you from?"*

Kashi was the name of their home planet. He slumped his shoulders, tried to look miserable. *It is hard to remember*, he replied. Vani appeared sympathetic.

Eric almost burst out laughing when he saw Strem walk into the ladies' rest room first. Strem was in and out of the door in a flash. When he finally returned, he was smiling. Mission accomplished.

"They're just like the ones on Earth," he whispered.

They entered a circular glass elevator along with a dozen other people and headed "up" toward the axis. In the cramped quarters a Kaulikan accidently hit Vani's arm, making her gasp. The gentleman quickly apologized. Eric figured the bone was probably broken. Too bad he couldn't take her to *Excalibur*; it could be put under the Healer and repaired in an hour.

The farms took up the equivalent of a dozen of the other low-ceilinged levels, curving up and away in both directions, clearly encircling the entire wheel. The agricultural plots were supported on layers of open platforms and scaffolds. Eric wouldn't have wanted to be around if they got hit with a meteor. The whole place would probably come crashing down. They appeared to be entering a fruit-tree section, except none of the trees were taller than knee-high.

As the elevator opened there was a significant increase in the honey odor Eric had initially noticed. Vani led them away from the others, along a narrow gully flowing with a thick translucent gel. They were up on the midlevels and Eric was thankful for the handrails. The nearby fruits were as hairy as miniature coconuts, only they were shaped as though they were inverted pears, with the stem fitting out of the heavy end.

"*Would you like one?*" Vani asked.

"*Ki,*" Eric said. Vani broke off three, one for each of them, and Strem quickly took a bite and almost cracked his teeth; they were rock-hard. Vani gave her now familiar puzzled expression and banged her fruit on the railing. The husk split, she pulled it off and threw it into the soil. Eric followed her example and was rewarded with the taste of another sugar-saturated delicacy. Strem threw his whole fruit away.

"*I planted these,*" Vani said. "*I attend to these plots.*"

Eric told her they were very good. He scowled at Strem.

Suddenly, loud chimes filled the air and people everywhere stopped what they were doing. Eric was still uncertain how to read Kaulikan emotions but there was no mistaking the sudden heaviness in the air. The forward and backward walls began to unravel as their numerous panels tilted edge on, like the opening of window blinds that could still be found in houses on Earth. Space was outside, and the ship's other two massive wheels, both of whose walls were also opening, turned in unison with them before the snowy nebula of the heart of The Milky Way. And in the other direction, beyond the hot spear of the ion drive, was the nova, whose bright light shone across the farm, seeming to cause the rows of plants to stand up and take notice. The chimes halted.

"*Dawn,*" Vani said. "*I used to cherish it.*"

The translation did not convey the sadness in her tone, but Eric didn't need the computer's help. Other shades of Kaulikan emotion could be misunderstood. Strange how sorrow seemed a thing above confusion.

"*Would you like to go elsewhere?*" she asked.

Eric glanced at Strem, whose expression was also easy to read. *Let's go to engineering,* he told her.

The elevator they took to the central shaft was different from the others; it was padded from top to bottom. Eric was glad he hadn't finished his lunch. As they rose through the levels, his weight dropped rapidly, until a deep breath was enough to bobble him off the floor.

Strem appeared perfectly at ease, however, and Vani was quickly regaining her good cheer.

The transfer point between the rotating wheel and the stationary axis was fascinating in its simplicity. This time a door in the ceiling of the elevator opened above them, which made sense when considering the physics of the setup. Eric remembered that his own people's first Earth space stations, before the advent of the graviton flux, had had similar peculiarities. All they had to do here was fly up and grab a pole that ran along a wide cushioned wall. Once he had hold of the pole his perspective was immediately set straight, and it was clear it was the elevator that was really moving. He watched as it curved overhead and disappeared.

"Do you have your bands?" Vani asked.

Their cute escort had wrapped an elastic strip of cloth around her forehead, holding her floating hair out of her face. Eric shook his head and began to spin like a top. Vani laughed.

"There will be bands with the scooter packs," she said, pulling herself smoothly along the pole. Eric followed at her feet—her slippers were not unlike his own, he noted—admiring the muscled curve of her calf through the hem of her pants. He accidently kicked Strem in the head.

They came to a cabinet that opened with the standard hand-to-the-light trick. The scooter packs fit on their backs and were designed to help them maneuver in the free fall. Eric was disappointed with their bulk and their obvious limited steering mechanism. He assumed they worked by the expulsion of compressed air; it wouldn't due to use rockets inside. Fortunately, there were headbands, and they were able to get their wigs out of their eyes.

A cavelike opening was nearby, and they entered

into a dark cavern. This was the first part of the ship they'd seen where space was freely squandered. Perhaps the area had held supplies that had already been consumed or else transferred to another part of the fleet.

They hooked onto a lit-up pulley system, and as Eric's eyes began to adjust, he realized they were traversing the end of a tank that appeared to run all the way to the front of the ship. Was the majority of the central shaft nothing but a fuel container? he wondered. With each passing year, the tank would be less full. They might travel all the way to another system, arriving only after generations had lived and died in the cold depths, and fail to find an inhabitable planet. And they would be out of fuel.

As the sides began to disappear they switched pulleys and directions, heading for the rear of the ship. A low pulse began to throb the nocturnal air. What light there was came from the other side of a complex metal lattice up ahead. The edges began to reappear as the axis narrowed. Vast networks of pipes knit the walls, around which Kaulikan men and women hummed on their scooters. All this equipment, Eric thought, maintained by thousands, and the hyper drive fit in a desk and needed a tune-up every ten years.

The pulley deposited them at the tip of an edifice that would have been a dangerous place to be had there been gravity. It was time for their backpacks. While Vani activated her jets, steering by a knob that fit in the palm of her hand, and floating effortlessly forward, Strem inadvertently turned his scooter on full and went rocketing past at a frightful speed.

Vani reacted instantly, accelerating and joining his tumbling body in midair. She was able to stabilize Strem and redirect his pack's nozzles, thus counteracting his forward momentum. Eric thought this was a remarkable feat considering her injured arm. He inched to where Strem hovered sheepishly. Vani looked more puzzled than ever.

"Have you two used scooters before?"

They were alone in a tunnel that led to a beehive of machines and people. The throbbing had deepened, making it necessary to speak loudly. *"Ki,"* Eric said.

Vani considered for a moment. *"Wouldn't you rather visit our garden? You must have heard that it is one of the most beautiful in all the worlds."*

Strem insisted, going through the initial muttered English routine, that he wanted to see engineering. To Vani, he must have sounded like a beast.

"Which world are you two from?"

Sammy had prepared them for this question, and Eric gave her an appropriate designation, a combination of letters and numerals. She did not know everything about every ship and therefore did not press the point. But they were not yet out of the woods.

"Engineering is always the same, always noisy. Why do you want to visit there?"

Eric told her that since they were so close, they would like to see it before going onto the garden. It was an answer that really wasn't an answer.

"I believe I should find you an escort that is fluent in Lutz. You would enjoy your visit more."

That wouldn't do at all. Eric racked his brain for a good reason why they should stay together. All he could come up with was a line about her company being more enjoyable than anything another might be able to show them.

Were compliments rare among the Kaulikan? Her face filled with a huge smile. Was it possible, by her people's standards, that she was ugly, and seldom received male attention? Vani never again mentioned another escort and seemed to hover closer to him as they continued their exploration.

Engineering overloaded Eric with its complexity. After the tour he was left with only a few clear impressions: giant black coils made up of wire thicker than a man's body, housed in transparent cylinders fanned with sparkling gases; computer boards larger than the *Excalibur* itself, registering with mazes of oscillating lights every discharge of the coils; and crackling bolts of artificial lightning, seen through filtered viewing portals that must have been several feet thick, arcing far out into space, generating the purple ion waves they had first glimpsed from hundreds of millions of miles away. It was from here the thunderous pulse originated, and for the Kaulikans to go on, it would have to beat a long, long time.

Even Strem was astounded by the machinery and for a while was content to watch and wait. Then suddenly, while they were pulling themselves around the belly of one of numerous spheric tanks, he pulled Eric aside. Vani continued forward, unaware.

"We've tasted the food and seen some of the sights," Strem said. "Let's hit her with the game question."

"Go ahead."

Strem frowned. "For some reason, which probably has to do with her extraterrestrial vision, she seems drawn to you. The question will sound less suspicious coming from you."

Eric glanced toward Vani, who was beginning to look over her shoulder, floating against the backdrop of a wide net of fiber optics. "Sammy, how is the thermometer?" he asked.

("So far, not bad, though it continues to creep up. But let me warn you, it won't heat up at a steady pace. At one point, it will take off.")

"We can't waste any more time," Strem said.

Vani was waiting patiently at a distance, understanding that they wanted to talk alone. Had the situation been reversed, had they been Kaulikans trying to penetrate an Earth station, they could never have come so far. Earth people were much more demanding of *appropriate* behavior.

"Are you having fun?" Eric asked.

"What kind of question is that?" Strem said.

"You were hoping to find excitement outside the web. Well, what have we got here?"

"I'm the captain of this mission. I can't enjoy myself until I know *Excalibur* is safe."

Eric sighed. "Yeah, you're right."

What was wrong with him? He was purposely prolonging the emergency. Curiosity was not a good enough excuse. Neither was a pretty face. They should get the coolant and leave. *Vani!* he called.

A blast of her scooter brought her back. He stopped her with his arm, touching her waist. She smiled. *"Have you seen enough of this noisy place?"*

No, he said, *Strem works with the refrigerator and cooling systems on our world and he's interested in seeing your world's systems.*

"But will they not be the same as yours?" Engineering was obviously not one of her favorite places to be.

Each world, Eric said, *has its own unique way of carrying out certain tasks. Strem wants to see your personnel in action.*

Vani gave Strem a curious look. *"All right."*

She took them to a fairly large chamber full of pipes, pumps, and people, and where there was an unmistakable chemical smell in the air—ethylene glycol. Vani noticed Strem's excitement. He pointed her toward a tank that bulged from a corner. It was all so perfect, Eric knew there had to be a catch. There was a valve that could be opened with a handle. Strem turned it slightly. A tiny dribble of coolant bubbled out. Then a bell began to ring. Every head in the room turned. A Kaulikan gentleman shot over. Vani intercepted him and there followed a brief discussion. The guy's message was clear: don't mess with the valves. The man turned off the alarm and returned to his station. Eric could see Strem counting the number of people in the chamber. He could read his thoughts: only eight measly Kaulikans. Strem looked at him, and Eric shook his head.

"*Is this what you wanted to see?*" Vani asked.

Eric nodded and inquired if there was another place where they stored ethylene glycol.

"*I do not know. Does Strem not know?*"

Are people always on duty here? he asked.

"*Of course.*"

"I want to speak to you alone, Eric," Strem said.

Eric excused themselves. They flew into an unoccupied corner. Vani must be getting some pretty weird ideas about them, thought Eric. But maybe there wasn't any crime in Kaulikan society, and she couldn't conceive of someone having unethical motives.

Strem didn't beat around the bush. "I wish you'd brought a gun."

"It won't work. You heard how the alarm sounds."

"And I saw where it turns off."

"You can't just shoot these people!"

"They'll wake up."

"You don't know that for sure. Their nervous systems are different. You could kill them."

"Nah. What are the chances of that? I can take out all eight of these people in a few seconds. I say we do it now."

"You're forgetting, there's nine people."

"It makes no difference."

"How can you say that after all the help she's given us?"

Strem groaned. "I understand that you like her. I like her myself. But we have a responsibility to our friends, and to Earth. We've got to get *Excalibur* out of here."

"Yeah, the Kaulikans might steal our secrets and attack Earth," he said sarcastically.

"They might. Not now. Not in the next ten years. But one day, who knows? Why do you think The Patrol hasn't helped them?"

He hesitated, thrown off balance by the question. "They don't know they're here."

"Don't fool yourself."

Strem was making a very interesting point; the truth of it had not occurred to Eric. The Patrol had hundreds of cruisers with which they scouted the borders of The Tachyon Web. From Sammy's brother, they knew The Patrol had been fully aware of the nova. Given that, The Patrol must have known of Kashi and its people. They must have been watching when the nova's fury hit the planet.

They must have watched and done nothing, while all those people died.

"We don't even know how to get back to the right air lock," he said.

"Sammy?" Strem said.

("I've tracked you closely. I know exactly where you are in relationship to . . . what was that?")

There had been a sudden burst of static.

"You tell us," Strem said.

("It's stopped. It must have been some kind of interference. Probably some equipment near you guys is radiating tachyons.")

"We were right on top of their ion drive and we didn't have interference," Strem said. "Could they be monitoring our transmissions?"

"We're on a supralight band," Eric said. "They don't have the technology."

"I don't like this," Strem said. "Even if they can't monitor our communications, we've got a spaceship stuck to their hull. Someone is bound to spot it soon. Let's get this over with." He reached inside his coat. Eric stopped him.

"This is crazy! We'll have to get past hundreds before we could get to the air lock."

"If we take care of these people right, there'll be no one to blow the whistle."

"You promised you wouldn't use your gun unless you were forced to." Eric glanced at Vani, who smiled and waved. "Sammy?" he said desperately.

("I'm open to any reasonable alternatives.")

("Just do it," Cleo said. "Sitting out here waiting for this thing to blow up beneath us is no fun. These people are so laid back. You'll have no trouble.")

"You're outvoted," Strem said.

("No, he's not!" Jeanie said. "Strem, you can't blast these people. What have they done to us?")

"I won't hurt them!" Strem repeated, exasperated. "I just want their damn coolant! And I'm not going to ask for it." He pulled out his gun, checking the charge. He added, "I'm the captain."

"You're the nephew of the owner of a broken-down freighter!" Eric said. "I don't have to take your orders!" He fought to control his temper. "Look, so Vani doesn't know where else coolant is stored. They must have it all over the ship. Maybe even back at the farms."

"I didn't see any there."

"We really didn't look. Doesn't it make more sense to try to get the stuff in a quiet place closer to the air lock?"

"You're the one who wanted to go to engineering!"

"That's before I knew they had alarms hooked up to their valves!"

"That's before you had a crush on Green Eyes!"

Eric stared him in the eye. "Don't push me, *Captain*."

Strem backed down. "We're getting nowhere," he growled.

"We have time," Eric said, trying to sound reasonable. "Let's explore further. I'm confident we'll find another source of coolant. We'll keep our eye on *Excalibur*'s temperature. If the situation gets critical, we'll return here and take our chances."

Strem chewed on that for a moment. "Having *Excalibur* spotted worries me as much as the graviton drive's heat. I want a time limit on this plan. Three hours. If we don't find the goods by then, we're coming back here, no matter what Sammy's thermometer says."

"Agreed," Eric said, reluctantly.

"And we're splitting up. That way, we can cover twice the ground. I don't need an escort. All I need to know is how to say *boo* and keep walking."

"I think that's a bad idea."

"And I think you'd rather be alone with her."

Eric had no smart answer. Strem was right.

9

They sat alone by a lake in the largely empty Kaulikan
garden. The solitude was internal as well as external.
Sammy had switched Strem's communicator to another
channel, and Eric was no longer having to endure Strem's
constant flippant remarks. Sammy had also agreed,
under protest, to stop monitoring Eric's every word
with Vani. He received his required Kaulikan responses
directly from *Excalibur*'s computers, and Sammy had
promised that they were no longer being broadcast over
the bridge's audio. Sammy could still call him, however, whenever he wanted, and vice versa.

The garden was on the same level as the farms but
was located in the forward wheel. Here, again, the
Kaulikans had spent their precious space freely, planning wisely for the claustrophobic centuries to come.
Though the species of grass, plants, and trees were
alien, Eric was surprised at how much he felt as if he
were in a forest on Earth; of course, everything was
green. One type of tree, however, if it was a tree, had
him wondering. They were as tall as Sequoias, but

didn't have bark or leaves, and their branches appeared to be covered with *hives*. With flowers everywhere, even floating in the clear lake water, he had to wonder if there was a Kaulikan inhabitant he had yet to meet. Where there were hives there were usually insects.

The architects had not forgotten the sky: a light—probably blue—canopy whose near horizons curved up rather than down. Perhaps the designers had even managed to manufacture the illusion of rain clouds. But because the wall plates were still tilted edge on, the stars were visible, and illusions were all they could be. The rays of the nova cast long shadows across the woods.

Eric had not yet found any coolant. Ninety minutes had elapsed since he had fought with Strem. He would have to start searching again, in a minute. . . .

"You are different, Eric, than anyone I know," Vani said.

How so? he asked.

They were sitting cross-legged on a boulder that seemed to be a hundred percent genuine rock. Vani leaned over and plucked what resembled a lotus from the lake, playing with the petals. *"Your face is unlike any I have ever seen."*

Is that good or bad? he asked.

In reply her left hand made a beautiful series of swirls.

My eyes, he said, *are still not working as they should. Please use words instead of fingers.*

"Your face has many thoughts in it that I do not understand." She looked him over. *"Even your clothes are different."*

You're different, he said, *from any girl I know.*

Vani laughed, not noticing his seriousness. *"My study period starts soon,"* she said suddenly.

Do you have to go?

Breaking the discipline had apparently never occurred to her. *"It is nice to sit here in the garden."*

Tell me, he said, *what you do each day?*

"But you know."

He shook his head. *My world is structured differently than yours.*

"I live in society's sector. We are all on the second rotation so we all get up at the same time. Recently, it seems, we have been getting up earlier and earlier, though I know that has not been so. But I have been tired."

Society's sector sounded like a dorm to Eric. He nodded for her to continue.

"Then we do our exercise."

What kind?

"The usual." She paused, dumbstruck. *"Do you not do your exercise?"*

Occasionally, he replied.

She laughed. *"But I know you eat. I saw you do that. And that is what I do next. Then I start on my shift. I mainly take care of the Silama. I make sure the impurities are removed before irrigation."*

Silama must be a word that had no English equivalent or else the computer would have given him an approximation, Eric thought. He asked if she liked her job.

"I do it." She did not understand the question.

Is there something else you would rather do?

"It is pleasant to watch the fruits grow and to know I was able to help them. I would not like to work where Durgi does, in the yeast factory. It is noisy there." She smiled. *"Like engineering."*

What are you going to do when you get older? he asked.

His probing was a surefire way of emphasizing their

separate origins. But it wasn't that his curiosity was getting the better of him, he realized. He *wanted* to tell her where he was from.

"*I will treat the Silama,*" she answered hesitantly. "*Unless I am transferred.*" She paused. "*Sometimes I wish that . . .*"

He had to prod her to complete the thought. She tossed her flower into the air. The gravity, half that of the rim of the wheel, brought it down gently into the water.

"*I wish that things were as they once were on Kashi. Not like when we were there, but as they were long ago, when our people used to walk outside beneath the sun. I always wanted to be in a real forest, in the mountains, and look out and see far away. Do you ever dream of those days, Eric?*"

In answer, he described to her his last backpacking trip when he had gone to the Himalayas, camped out on a glacier, scaled a sheer cliff without a graviton pack, and enjoyed a glorious view of the sunset from the top of Mt. Everest. He was not trying to add to her confusion, rather, he simply wanted to share the experience. And she seemed to understand, though she could not possibly have known what he was talking about.

"*Those are some of the strange thoughts I see in your face. When you go to these places, are you always alone?*"

He had in fact been alone on the trip. He nodded, and then asked about her friends.

"*All those in my society are friendly.*"

Were any of them special to her? he wanted to know.

"*Durgi and I spent many of our breaks together. I was unhappy when she was transferred. But we knew this would happen on her twenty-second cycle. Other than she, I don't really have any special friends.*"

Does everyone get transferred on their twenty-second cycle?

This question struck her funnier than any of his others. *"Not always, not if their mate works in the same sector. Surely it must be the same on your world?"*

So they got married when they were twenty-two, and their relationships were monogamous. This was quite a change from the way things were back home these days. Sammy had said Kashi revolved around its sun in less than three hundred days; therefore, their cycles were probably less than an Earth year.

How many cycles are you? he asked.

"Twenty-one." She stared at him a moment, then reached for another flower. *"You look more than twenty-two."*

He nodded. He probably was.

She brushed the flower against her cheek. *"Who are you coupled to?"*

No one.

"You were unable to choose?"

In a way.

"But did not the Council select someone for you?"

No.

"But when you do not choose, the Council always selects. It is the law."

He did not want to lie to her. *My world is different than yours,* was all he could think of to say.

This time the line did not satisfy her; she fidgeted on the boulder. He glanced down at his opant jacket. He did not have to let the cat out of the bag but maybe he could show its tail. He removed the coat and pressed the hidden on-switch beneath the collar. The jacket began to glow. She stared, amazed, hesitating to put it on until he reassured her that it was safe. As he was considerably bigger than she and since she couldn't put her injured arm through the right sleeve, the fit was loose, but good enough to allow the coat's sensors to get a grip on her emotions. Were his motives entirely pure? he wondered. She was unaware that the opant could give him a Peeping Tom's insight into her feelings, maybe even her feelings about him. But he was spared a dose of guilt when he realized the green contacts made it impossible to assess the jacket's shades of color; he could only see variations in the brightness of the light.

"*This is pretty,*" she said, excited. "*How is it that the colors move?*"

They move with your feelings, he said. *Think of what makes you happy.*

"*Landing on Lira.*"

Lira must be their destination. *Okay, pretend you're there,* he said.

Eric suddenly saw the light begin to change, though he was not sure in which direction.

"*Now the jacket is blue. It works as you say. But how? We have no clothes like this on our world.*"

Blue must be happiness for Kaulikans, and not yellow, like it was for Earth people, he thought.

Vani was impressed. "*One day, I must visit your world. It must be very different.*"

That would be nice, he thought, feeling sad that he must continue to deceive her. She continued to marvel at the beauty of the jacket. He asked if it was hurting her arm.

"*No.*"

How did you break it?

The opant light changed, getting dimmer, less uniform. Bad question. "*I fell off a ladder in the farm. A few days ago.*" Her voice lowered. "*It was dawn, and I was looking at the sun and it was bright, so bright . . .*

and I fell." She forced a smile. *"Now I am like you, I do not do my exercise."*

Does it hurt? he asked.

"Not now." She touched her injured arm. *"But I have not slept much since then. I guess it does hurt."*

It was not her arm that was keeping her awake. It was the damn nova, and what it had done. *The jacket is yours,* he said. *Keep it.*

"But I cannot. It was issued to you."

I've got thousands of them.

"You are so different. Why is it your world wanted you to visit ours?"

They didn't. We just came, he said.

"But how? Why?"

I can't say.

"Did one of the Councils send you?"

No.

A peculiar expression crossed Vani's face. *"Are you in the Guard?"*

That sounded ominous, though it would have been foolish to assume the Kaulikans had no security personnel. He shook his head and told her he didn't know much about the Guard, hoping she might tell him what she knew.

"I have never met any of them myself, not that I know of, and I have never heard First Councillor Rak speak of them. But Durgi once said she knew a man who was a member of the Guard. She only spoke to him a few times and was not sure exactly what he did, other than that he helped insure the safety of the worlds."

Eric had no trouble imagining what a member of the Guard did. Watching over delicate facilities such as engineering had to be at the top of their list. He'd better tell Strem about this—soon.

"If you are not in the Guard, what do you do in your world?" she asked.

I study.

"What do you study?"

How people would be different if they came from other stars, he said, *and how they would be the same.*

Vani nodded. *"Our program is concentrating on similar material. We study about the stars; how they are formed; how far away they are."* She held up the arm of the opant, marveling at the flowing colors. *"We study why it is that nothing can ever go faster than light."*

That's not true, he said. *Anything can go anywhere in no time if it knows how.*

"But the tapes say . . ."

Never mind what the tapes say, he interrupted.

Vani was not one to argue. *"Sometimes, I have also thought that way."*

She turned, pointing toward the far forward wall and the tilted panels, into space. Directly out from the nose of the ship's central shaft, a bright star shone against a dark galactic dust cloud. *"Sometimes, I watch Lira before I fall asleep, and it does not look so far away."*

He suspected, given the Kaulikans' technology, that they would know if Lira had orbiting planets, but that they wouldn't know if the planets were inhabitable or not. If only he had the coolant, a few pounds of cheap chemicals, he could go there and be back in less than an hour with a full report. But even then, would news of a lush world be of any help? It would be a world she would never know. . . .

With each passing minute, he was moving closer to telling her the truth. He came to his senses when he imagined what Strem and the others would do to him if he did tell. And he was afraid that Vani would think he was crazy.

I believe, Eric said, *we could reach Lira in the blink of an eye*.

She laughed at his wishful thinking. "*And the top of a mountain?*"

He nodded and said, *Wherever we wanted to go*.

She bopped him on the head with her flower. "*I like you, Eric*."

"And I like you, Vani," he said in English, not giving her the translation automatically supplied by his implant. He took her flower, fitted it in her hair by her ear, and smiled; she knew what he meant.

The chimes he had heard earlier at the farm returned. The wall panels began to fold down. With the light of the nova cut off, the garden settled into a gentle twilight, the sky emitting but a faint glow.

Vani stood and offered her good hand. Her skin was much softer than his, warmer, and he waited nervously for her to comment on the roughness of his touch. She said nothing. She was leading him along a stony path toward a waterfall that poured out the side of the tall hived trees. The land was curving upwards toward an artificial heaven it would never reach, while outside the black windows the real universe waited. The smell of honey was almost intoxicating. And Vani liked him. How silly it sounded to travel uncountable miles into the unknown and to have as his greatest discovery someone who cared about him. He laughed at the thought.

"*What's so funny?*" she asked.

Eric squeezed her hand. *Nothing, Vani*, he replied. But what if she knew he was an alien?

They stopped close enough to the waterfall to feel its

spray and found another smooth rock, sitting and dangling their feet above a foaming pool a hundred feet below. Eric's thoughts were returning reluctantly to the three-hour deadline when suddenly a *creature* landed on his shoulder, startling him, almost causing him to jump over the edge. Vani had let go of his hand, but quickly grabbbed his arm. Then she laughed.

"The Sila like you. That is rare."

A cross between a butterfly and a small bird was sitting not six inches from his face, peering at him with a triangle of three warm eyes. The wings were standing straight up, together, beautifully patterned, obviously insectile. The body was coated with a mammal's fine fur. A tubelike snout protruded a couple of inches out from where the mouth should have been. Earth's genetic laboratories would have had trouble conjuring up this one.

Eric swallowed and shook slightly. The Sila took a hop closer and stuck its snout in his ear. Either it had spotted his implant or else it just liked wax. Vani was delighted.

"A Sila has never done that to me. How does it feel?"

It tickles, he said. The computer had not translated Silama or Sila. Clearly there was a connection between the words. He watched as more of the creatures, one by one, flew out of the huge hived tree, alighting on the flowers. They'd been waiting for the windows to close. He assumed the Sila were removing pollen from the flowers and transforming it into Silama. He could envision pipes inside the tree pumping the honeylike final product over to the farms. No wonder all the food tasted like it was saturated with sugar. The Silama must be like a potent fertilizer.

Vani couldn't get over the little critter's attraction

to him. *"I have not seen this happen with anyone since I was with Belri."*

Who is Belri? he asked.

"My brother. The Sila loved him. No one knew why."

Where is he? he asked, foolishly, not reading the signs. The opant light had shifted once again. Vani began to kick her dangling feet, looking down where the waterfall crashed over the rocks.

"He is not here."

Does he live on another world?

She hesitated. *"Yes."*

Do you ever see him?

"We exchanged tapes last week." She paused, a mild tremor going through her body. *"He lived on Kashi."*

Eric could have kicked himself for being so slow. Belri was dead. He may even have been one of the countless people they'd seen catch fire and turn to ash on the Kaulikan news broadcast.

"All my family was on Kashi. I was the only one picked to go. I was the youngest. I was told I was fortunate. The greatest adventure, they said. I knew the sun was in trouble, but I do not think I really understood. Had I understood, I probably would have stayed." She caught herself, struggling with her emotions. He half expected tears but maybe it was that Kaulikans didn't cry. *"I am sorry. We have all left someone behind. Even First Councillor Rak had to leave his family. You have your own burdens. I did not want to give you mine."*

He felt like a hypocrite. Strem and he were the only ones aboard the ship who had not suffered. He wanted to comfort her, but he had no sense of the Kaulikans' philosophy of life and death, or of their religion, if they even had one. All he could do was sit stupidly, feeling his guilt deepen. Vani ran her fine fingers through the moist sandy soil beside the rock on which they rested.

"I did not speak my thoughts clearly. Sometimes I do wish I had remained on Kashi, but usually I am glad that I am here. There will be no adventure for me, I know now. I will die before the stars can begin to change. But I will have children, if it is permitted, and they too will have children. And one day, some day . . ." her voice trailed off and she held up a fistful of the soil, letting it slip slowly through her fingers into the rushing waters below. *"And my ashes will still be here. I will grow and be in everything."* She forced a wry smile his way. *"Maybe I will be a flower, and the Sila will like me, as they like you, and liked Belri."*

He put his arm around her shoulder and she leaned into him. The feel of her hair against his cheek was wonderfully soft. He might have kissed her then, or tried to, but suddenly, Sammy spoke in his ear.

("Eric, I must talk to you.")

"Yes?" he whispered. Vani was entirely used to him muttering to himself in a nonsensical language before he spoke to her in Kaulikan. But this time she waited and he said nothing to her.

("If you are with Vani, excuse yourself. You and I are going to get into an argument.")

Apprehensive, he let go of Vani and stood. *I have to be alone for a few moments*, he told her. Thankfully, she did not ask him why. He hurried down the stone path and around a thick hedge. The roar of the waterfall lessened.

"What's Strem up to?" he asked. "It hasn't been three hours."

("The temperature is way up, in the critical zone.")

"Have you tried the filtered coolant?"

"(I'm afraid to.)"

"Did this just happen?"

("No. We started heating up rapidly about an hour ago.")

"But why didn't you tell me?"

("Eric, I have not been monitoring your talks with Vani, but I have been tracking you. For the last hour, you have remained in one area. You have not been searching for coolant.")

"That's not true!" Actually, it was a perfectly accurate statement.

("Strem asked me not to tell you. I had to agree with some of his reasons.")

"*His* reasons? What were they?"

("He's going to take the coolant from that place in engineering that Vani showed you. He's going to stun the personnel on duty. He was afraid if you knew, you would try to stop him. But I decided I should call you now to tell you to start making your way back to the air lock where you stowed your pressure suit. Strem's going to be in a hurry when he leaves and I don't want him to have to go looking for you.")

"He won't be in any kind of hurry! How, with forty gallons of ethylene glycol over his back?"

("This is what we're going to argue about. Cleo and Jeanie have put on Kaulikan costumes and entered the ship. They're with Strem now in engineering. They are going to help him carry out the coolant.")

"Have you gone as mad as he? You're risking the girls? I can't believe it!"

("We were risking the girls by doing nothing. They wanted to go, or at least Cleo did. Then Jeanie didn't want her to go alone.")

"Why didn't *you* go?"

("Believe me, I wanted to. I'd love to get a look at their engines. But I had to stay. I have to have *Excalibur* ready to leave the instant they get back.")

"But you know as well as I do that Jeanie won't use a gun."

("She brought one. Strem convinced her that we have no choice. He convinced me. The drive's getting real hot.")

"Let me talk to him."

("He said he doesn't want to talk to you.")

"I don't give a damn what he says! Put him on my channel now!" There was a slight crack of static in Eric's implant. "Strem?"

("Eric, my boy, how's your love life?")

"Listen to me, Strem, this isn't going to work. Vani told me about a Guard the Kaulikans have. They oversee sensitive areas like engineering."

("I didn't see any of this Guard. Did you, Eric?")

"No. But they're around. They probably monitor certain areas by remote camera."

("I knew you would start up like this. Look, buddy, get your tail back to the air lock. My two soldiers and I are not far from that fancy room with the big tanks of coolant. We'll have the stuff in a few minutes and then we'll join you.")

"You don't believe me."

("Well, now that you mention it . . .")

"Then ask Vani. They have a Guard!"

("So what if they do? We can take care of ourselves.")

"You have three stunners, for goodness sakes! There are a hundred thousand people in this ship. If an alarm is sounded, you'll never get out. Think, Strem; for once in your life, think hard. Jeanie and Cleo are with you. It's their lives you're risking."

("No, Eric, you've got it backwards. I'm trying to save their lives. And yours. Sammy, break this channel. I've got work to do. I can't have all these negative voices in my head.")

"Wait!"

There was another brief crack of static, and he was alone with Sammy on the band.

("Sorry, Eric. He needs to concentrate. His mind is set. Nothing you could have said would make any difference.")

"I guess you're right," he said with a sigh. "But do me a favor. Wish him good luck for me."

10

Vani rose when he returned to the waterfall, seeing his anxiety. *"What has happened?"* she asked.

He had only known her a few hours. Even though he knew she liked him, he couldn't very well tell her his partner was engaged in theft and expect her help. He simply told her he had to get to engineering as quickly as possible.

"Has something happened to Strem?"

Not yet, he said, *but he's in danger.*

"But how do you know?"

He let her peek inside his ear. *This is a communicator*, he explained. *Strem told me he's in danger.*

Vani questioned him no further, though the implant must have been as strange to her as the opant coat. They left the garden at a swift pace, catching a padded elevator leading directly to the central shaft. As his weight decreased, his tension increased. He didn't know what to hope for. If Strem and the girls got caught, they'd be in terrible trouble, and if they pulled it off, they'd be leaving the Kaulikans in the same mess as before. And he'd never see Vani again. It seemed he couldn't win.

The elevator ceiling opened and they dove into a cushioned area, complete with guiding poles, that was similar to the place they'd encountered on their first trip to the hub. But this time they were in the forward section, not the rear. As they donned scooter packs, Eric reemphasized the need for haste and indicated he wanted to use the jets at maximum velocity. At first Vani protested, saying it was not allowed, but when he insisted she led him out of the well-lit mattress area into a dark region beside a mammoth curving wall. His earlier guess had been correct. The forward portion of the shaft was essentially a fuel tank. Phosphorescent bands lined the giant container, stray Kaulikans drifting around its rim. Vani took Eric's hand, and they pressed the scooters' control knobs for top speed. Compressed air sprayed out their backs as they rocketed forward.

Wind whistled in their faces. It was as though they were falling down a deep well. People rushed by, some crying out for them to slow down. Twice they escaped what would have been serious collisions by inches. Vani's hair waved on the wind, and Eric could feel his wig loosening. And all the while, he was afraid he would be too late.

They left the fuel tank behind and plunged into the wide space where they had previously caught the pulleys. Vani motioned to turn the scooters around. The cave's walls of pipes became visible as they braked forcibly. There was a moment of panic for Eric when he doubted they could stop in time, but by the time they reached the web of girders that encased engineering, they were coasting at a relaxed speed. The throb of the ion drive filled his ears. They landed on the same edifice as before, but on this trip he had to go on alone. Vani did not like that idea.

"I can help your friend Strem. You will need me to find him."

Eric assured her he knew his way and that she could do him the most help by waiting in this exact spot. She began to protest, but he was firm. As he turned to go up the tunnel, he hugged her briefly. "Don't go away," he said in English.

Of course he got lost. He was drifting aimlessly along a row of the sparkling coils wrapped in their gaseous cases when he decided it was time to call Sammy. "I've gone to engineering instead of the air lock. How close am I to our SWAT team?"

("How did you get to engineering so fast?")

"I flew. Where are they?"

("They've already entered the chamber. You're too late.")

"Where are they?"

("Facing the rear of the ship, they are at ten o'clock, eighty-five yards from you and slightly forward. Don't interfere, Eric.")

Eric reoriented himself and, using handles fixed to a pipe that was going his way, pulled his weightless body toward the coolant chamber. But all of a sudden he began to slow. He *was* too late. Strem was going to use force, and there would be no talking him out of it now. And if Strem and the girls did get caught, what good could Eric Tirel do keeping them company in jail?

"Sammy, can you switch me onto Strem's channel? Please?"

("He's even switched me off. He wants the three of them totally focused on what they're doing.")

"Do you still have video?"

("Yes. Strem has positioned them in separate corners. The people on duty are beginning to wonder what's going on.")

Eric rounded a loud pump and spotted a circular opening in the ceiling that he remembered led to the room with the coolant. One hard push and he could be in the middle of the action. He stayed where he was.

"Sammy?"

("They're reaching for their guns.")

"What kind of shot is Cleo?"

("She shot at me with a stunner once. She didn't miss. Oh, no.")

"What is it?"

("Jeanie is losing her nerve. She's shaking her head, putting down her gun. Strem's shouting something, I don't know what.")

Faintly, Eric could hear the shout: "Now!"

He couldn't bear it any longer. He launched himself toward the round door, catching the rim of the entrance with his outstretched hands. Peeking over the edge, he saw a flash of light striking a Kaulikan in the chest, sending him toppling. Strem was the marksman.

The room erupted in dazzling beams, and Cleo joined the hunt. Jeanie, pressed into a corner, watched in frozen fright. One Kaulikan let out a cry and tried to grab Cleo. Pivoting smoothly in the free fall, she shot him directly in the face. There came another cry, but it was Strem shouting in victory. There had been ten Kaulikans on duty instead of the expected eight but it had made no difference. Moments after Strem had started the attack, the Earth people were the only ones left standing.

Strem put away his weapon and pulled out the inflatable container from beneath his shirt. Cleo fetched Jeanie from the corner. Eric, watching from less than forty yards away, couldn't utter a word. Strem placed

Cleo next to the alarm button and fit the mouth of the bag around the coolant nozzle. He turned the handle, and ethylene glycol began to expand the folded sack. The alarm remained silent. Cleo pulled out a second bag as Strem topped off the first. All was going as planned. The floating bodies were ignored.

Then something dreadful happened. The portal through which Eric was watching suddenly slammed shut, almost taking off his fingers. He backed away, feeling himself sinking inside. *Now* the alarm went off. But this was not some insignificant-sounding bell signaling that a valve had been accidently opened. This sound reverberated throughout the entire central axis, overriding the throb of the ion drive, a high-pitched ringing that could inspire panic in the guilty and the innocent alike.

"Sammy!"

("Get out of there!")

"But Strem . . . the girls . . ."

("I know, I know. But you can't stay. Get away. Come back here. We'll think of something . . . somehow.")

"I'm on my way," he said. He had warned them but he had also helped put them in the desperate state where they could not listen to his warning.

Eric took one last look at the locked portal, turned and activated his scooter. He headed for the tunnel through which he had entered engineering. Kaulikans were moving toward the coolant chamber in waves, among them a few darkly clad individuals he was almost sure were members of the Guard. They ignored him—why shouldn't they? Eric remembered Vani—and all was not lost. He was returning to *Excalibur* but not before he got what they had come for.

Vani was still waiting where Eric had left her. The

alarm had obviously been hard on her nerves. The ringing halted just as he spotted her at the end of the tunnel and she flew toward him, embracing him with her good arm much harder than he had hugged her when he had said good-bye minutes before. The cessation of the bell did not reassure him. If Kaulikan security mistakenly believed their people had been killed, instead of knocked unconscious, who could blame them if they reacted violently?

"*What has happened?*" Vani cried. "*Where is your friend?*"

He indicated he had to speak through his communicator. Looking out over the void between engineering and the fuel tank, he could see flocks of Kaulikans materializing out of the inky darkness. All of a sudden they didn't look like such peaceful people.

"Sammy?"

("They're trying to cut through the door.")

"It's two-feet thick!"

("It's melting.")

Seeing the stunners transformed into high-energy generators would not help alleviate the Guard's paranoia. "Have you been able to talk to them?"

("Not really. Strem keeps cursing, and Jeanie's crying and Cleo . . . I don't know what Cleo's doing.")

"Patch me in."

("Right away.")

A hissing buzz shook his ears, overlayed with heavy breathing and obscene language—the lasers and Strem. "Strem, this is Eric."

("Damnit, this stuff is harder than these people should be able to make! Yeah, buddy, I know, you told me so. Cleo, stay focused on that one spot!")

"I haven't called to criticize you."

("Man, that's a relief. I feel a whole lot better now.")

"Strem, you're trapped, face it. Put the guns down. Their Guard must be watching you this second. If you make it clear that you're surrendering, that they can take you without force, things will go much easier for all of you."

("I'm not surrendering! I'll be through this door in five minutes!")

"By that time, there will be five thousand waiting to greet you on the other side."

Strem's voice was low. ("Did you see them?")

"They're on their way. The charges in your guns must be getting pretty low."

("But if we give up . . .")

"If you don't give up, they'll kill you. And Cleo. And Jeanie."

There was a long pause. ("Cleo, stop, turn it off. Shh, Jeanie, don't worry, we'll be all right.") The buzzing ceased. ("Okay, Eric, we're putting down our weapons. Now what?")

"Just a minute." He turned his attention to Vani. Anxiety was another emotion that transcended planetary origins. Lines creased her brow, while other Kaulikans crowded past them in the tunnel, not realizing they were brushing shoulders with another of the wicked intruders. He pulled her to the side, along a thick beam.

"Please," she begged. *"You have a secret you must tell me."*

The truth would have to be administered in doses. He couldn't blow her mind with talk of hyper jumps and The Union, not when he needed her the most. He told her that Strem and two others of his friends had set off the alarm by trying to take forty gallons of coolant without permission. He did not mention the guns or the people they had stunned. Nevertheless, Vani was sufficiently shocked.

"*But if your world needs the fluid, why did not Strem put in a standard request?*"

Our world doesn't need the coolant, he said, *we need it.*

Vani looked around at the awful commotion he and his partners had started. "*What do you need it for?*"

To save lives.

"*I do not know where it is stored except in that room I showed you.*" She clasped her left hand around her injured arm, her whole body shaking. She wanted to help him, he could tell, but she was afraid.

I understand, he replied. *But you must know someone who works with the coolant, someone who could give it to you and not ask a lot of questions.*

She lowered her head. "*There is someone . . .*"

He knew from his earlier examination of the Kaulikans that they had a unit of measurement called a *squzz* that equaled approximately four gallons. He told her he needed ten squzz.

"*But you have not told me why. Do you not trust me?*"

He squeezed her shoulder. *Trust me, Vani*, he said.

She looked down at his hand, studying his calloused fingers, which were probably unlike any man's she had ever known. Something in her face seemed to change, to darken, and he wondered if she were beginning to guess the truth.

"*I will get you the coolant. But I must go for it alone. I will bring it back here.*"

Is the place you're going to in the axis, in free fall?

She was avoiding his eyes. "*No, it is at the farms.*"

But you won't be able to handle the weight. I must go with you, he said.

"*No. You are a stranger to this world. The alarm was*

*sounded by a stranger who was taking coolant. If you
are with me when I talk to my friend, he will ask
questions about you. This way is best."*

His suspicion left a bad taste in his mouth. He
couldn't help it. *How will you carry the ten squzz?*

*"I will find a cart. I should hurry before talk of this
spreads."*

The ideal move would be for her to take the coolant
directly to the air lock. But there were difficulties with
this plan. He did not know how to describe to her
exactly which air lock it was. He could give her his
implant and let Sammy guide her with the help of
Excalibur's translator, but then *he* wouldn't have an
implant. He'd be out of touch and might even get lost.
Plus, the implant, fitted in Vani's ear, might frighten
her further.

Could you bring the coolant to an air lock, he asked.

Now she looked at him, but it was a look of shock. *"You
are going to take it outside?"*

He nodded and pulled his inflatable bag from beneath his shirt. *Fill this with the ethylene glycol,* he said.
It holds approximately five squzz.

But she refused the bag. *"I can get a container that
will hold it all. Now I must go."*

She did not ask which air lock. That was a bad sign,
he thought. He asked her to be patient a moment
longer. He contacted Sammy. "I'm going to give her
my implant. You'll have to guide her. What do you
think?"

("Her excuses are logical. But I don't know—")

("Trust her," Strem interrupted.)

Had the situation been less desperate, Eric would
have laughed. "What's new at your end?"

("Now it's them that're trying to cut through the
door. We must have fused it shut.")

"Don't fight with them."

("I hope they don't believe in torture.")

"I have to say good-bye, now."

("Just in case she brings more than coolant to the air lock, Cleo left a gun in your pressure suit.")

"But you just said to trust her!"

("To a point. Hey, you got a plan to rescue us?")

"Yes," he lied. "A great plan. Sammy?"

("Go ahead, put it in her ear.")

"We'll all be together soon," he said, trying to sound like he believed it. He turned to Vani and told her he had another present for her. Pinching the tip of his ear up and away from his head with his thumb and index finger, he scraped inside the canal with the nail of his little finger. The implant popped out, a miniature silver oval, and floated in the air between them.

Vani took one look at it and shook her head, saying something he no longer had the means to understand. Eric reassured her the best he could with gestures. Finally, she nodded reluctantly and allowed him to jam the device in her ear canal, which was considerably narrower than his own. Suddenly, her eyes widened. Sammy must have said hello using the computer's mechanical voice. If anything, this seemed to make her more anxious to get away from him. There were no hugs this time.

Vani activated her scooter, and Eric watched as she glided toward the lit pulley bars and disappeared in the deeps of the central shaft. For a moment he contemplated following her. But, if she were going to betray him, he decided, he would rather know later than sooner. At least at the air lock he would have a chance of escape. With a quick look back in the direction where his friends were cornered, he shoved off to find the air lock.

*   *   *

Retracing his steps proved to be easier than he'd anticipated. Eric crossed the void between engineering and the fuel tank and found what he believed to be the elevator Vani had originally used to take them to the central shaft. It was empty and he took it all the way to the rim and was let out on a corridor that seemed to stretch forever. But Strem and he had been lucky with their choice of entrance, for the door to that particular air lock was only fifty yards from where the corridor had dead-ended in another elevator; it was not necessary for him to stop and peek in every room to see if it was the right one. At this recollection he could have kicked himself; he could have told Vani how to find the air lock and kept his communicator, after all. Yet, having Sammy's companion words in her head might have its advantages. That is, if she hadn't removed the implant the second she had gotten out of his sight.

The corridor had its pedestrians but none stopped to chat with him. He refrained from running, keeping a reasonable pace, occasionally nodding his head and muttering *boo*. This went on for ten minutes. Reflecting on how much distance he'd covered, Eric figured he'd circumvented almost the entire wheel. This didn't bother him, knowing it was better to be a long time heading in what he knew to be the right direction than to be lost on some shortcut. Finally, he spotted the end-of-the-line elevator and nonchalantly strode into the air-lock dressing room like it was his own sleeping quarters.

The lockers were jammed with *Excalibur*'s pressure suits. Except for the helmet, Eric put on all of his gear, getting ready for a quick exit. He sat down and waited, holding the gun Cleo had thoughtfully left behind. Vani was not going to betray him, he told himself. She cared about him. She would bring the coolant. She was a nice alien.

But he kept his finger on the trigger. It was fortunate that he was ready.

When thirty of the slowest imaginable minutes had passed, when he was beginning to think he'd better take a brief hike outside and check with Sammy on Vani's progress, the door suddenly burst open. Three Kaulikans were standing in the corridor: two men, one woman. The latter was dressed in black and was holding an object that was unmistakably designed for firing something at someone. Eric's reaction was not one of fear. He just felt sad, terribly sad. She had lied to him when he had been prepared to tell her the truth. She would never reach Lira. He was sad for her.

He had his gun resting on his knee, under his helmet.

"*Boo*," he said.

The woman motioned for him to stand and come out into the corridor. He could see immediately that the Kaulikan society was not practiced in police work. Seasoned disciplinaries would have had guns enough for all three of them and they would have been ready for the simple trick he pulled. He stood slowly, then abruptly dropped his helmet and shot the woman in the abdomen, the flash of the weapon knocking her backward. The two men froze in surprise, making easy targets. Another couple of squeezes of the trigger and they hit the floor beside their comrade.

The next meeting between human and Kaulikan civilization was already ruined. The golden girl of his dreams was gone. Next spring break, he was staying home.

He snapped on his helmet and stepped into the air lock, slamming the door at his back. The controls presented no problems, and he was able to crack the overhead hatch and allow the atmosphere to escape. He then climbed the ladder and manually unscrewed the hatch the remainder of the way, throwing it open and poking his head outside. The black vacuum and the cold stars were not a welcome sight. He flipped on his head lamp and stood up on the hull.

The hike to *Excalibur* was brief and painful. Eric really could not remember ever feeling so completely miserable in all of his life. It was no consolation that things were undoubtedly going to get worse before they got better. The familiar sight of *Excalibur* only brought a tinge of relief. Who could celebrate climbing into a time bomb? He stumbed into the freighter's air lock and pushed a button. Air gushed around his legs. He leaned against the wall. He was exhausted.

"What are you doing here?" Sammy yelled at him the moment he stepped into the cargo bay. Eric removed his helmet and immediately sneezed. After the sweet clean smells of the Kaulikan craft, Uncle Dan's pride and joy stunk.

"I was asking myself the same question." He put a hand to his head, feeling pressure inside and out. "Vani sent their Guard after me."

"No, she didn't!"

"She did. Never trust a girl with green eyes and white hair. Three of their people tried to arrest me in the air lock."

"Naturally, the Kaulikans started going through their air locks. But Vani didn't send them! She's on the line now. She's got the coolant. I was leading her to the right air lock when I heard you entering."

It was amazing how a little good news could pick him up. "Let me talk to her!"

"No. You have to go back to the air lock."

"I can't do that. I left three bodies lying in the corridor. How far is Vani from the air lock?"

"I've got her in an elevator heading toward the rim."

"Steer her toward another air lock. She'll freak when she sees what I've done to her people. I've got it. Send her in the opposite direction along the corridor. I'll take another implant and a spare pressure suit. You track us both and when we get atop each other, let me know and I'll look around for a hatch."

"You're going to take her aboard?"

"Yeah."

"Why?"

"I like her."

Sammy nodded. "Maybe we could use her as a hostage."

"What?"

"Sorry, another one of Strem's ideas. I've got to stop listening to that guy. The Guard has him and the girls. They've removed their contacts and wigs. They know we're from somewhere else. The Guard has also taken away their remote eyes on their belts so I'm unable to see where they are. But they've still got the implants in their ears. I can track them and talk to them."

"What's our ship's temperature?"

"Off the dial. You better go."

The secret was out of the bag. He could tell Vani the truth with a clear conscience. He grabbed a communicator and suit and went out the way he had come in. Eric felt a surge of energy and jogged along the dark gully cut by the rim of the wheel. With his fresh implant, he could have spoken to Vani, but he didn't want to confuse her with too many voices. Sammy could feed her directly with translated instructions.

He had passed three hatches when Sammy told him to stop. ("She's right beneath you," he said.)

Fortunately, the air lock was a duplicate of the other one, and he was inside and under atmosphere in minutes. Vani was in the locker room, standing beside a wheeled cart that held ten big bottles. She was a nervous wreck but she smiled for his benefit. He wanted to kiss her to thank her a thousand times over, and apologize for ever doubting her. Instead, he held up his spare pressure suit. She shook her head.

"I do not like being in the vacuum."

"Sammy, tell her it will only be for a minute. Then she will see something more wonderful than can be seen from any mountaintop."

Vani listened seriously to the whispered words in her head, then chuckled. *"But that was a dream."*

It was real, he had Sammy tell her.

She accepted the suit and he showed her how to put it on. The fit was lousy—it was too big and her broken arm didn't help matters—but it would last her the distance to *Excalibur*.

The air lock was not equipped with a lift. He had to carry the ten four-gallon bottles up onto the deck one by one. The cart, however, could be folded and he was able to fit it through the hatch, saving himself several backbreaking trips between the air lock and the ship.

When the two of them were assembled on the hull, the coolant at their feet, Vani began to have trouble maintaining her balance; the surroundings were eerie enough for Eric's star-traveled instincts, and she apparently didn't go outside often, if ever. He took hold of her good hand, worried how her injured arm was holding up without the sling, and they set off at a careful pace, the cart rolling smoothly over the metal floor. It occurred to him that he had not even checked to see if she had gotten the right stuff. He would have given a lot to be able to read her mind as the bulk of *Excalibur* began to loom out of the night.

She hesitated at the entrance to the air lock. But as

he began to unload the bottles, she stepped inside and leaned in a corner, supporting her wrist. She was scared but he could see a gleam in her eyes through the faceplate. He was praying that the whites in Sammy's eyes didn't frighten her. If they did, he wasn't taking off his contacts. Or his wig, for that matter.

Sammy was not there to greet them in the cargo bay. Strem and company must be keeping him busy, Eric thought. He pulled off his suit and helped Vani out of hers, once accidentally tugging on her sore arm, causing her to wince. She stared at the many stacked cartons and he pointed to her opant jacket.

See, I told you I had thousands of them, Eric said.

Yet, she did not understand what the strange ship and cargo meant. He lugged the coolant bottles to a capped pipe in the rear corner, then got Sammy on the intercom.

"Shall I pour it straight in?"

"By all means. Is it ethylene glycol?"

He popped the top of one of the containers, took a sniff. "A vintage year."

"I'm going to enjoy watching the temperature go down."

"I'll be up on the bridge in a minute." He added, "If Vani chokes when she sees your face, don't take it personally."

When he had the coolant safely circulating around the Preeze Cap, Eric led Vani toward the control room. Every nook and cranny fascinated her.

I have never seen a ship like this. Where are its rockets?

It doesn't have any.

"But how does it . . . ?"

She stopped. It was a tribute to her fine manners that she did not faint. Sammy, who must have been shaving while they'd been coming through the air lock, was clean-faced and trying to stand up straight, as he greeted her in the sleeping-quarters hallway.

"Boo," he said.

"Smile," Eric said.

Sammy smiled. Vani looked from each of them, back and forth, then slowly reached out and grasped Eric's white locks, pulling off his wig. He held his breath. She pointed to his eyes, as if to say, the same as your friend's? He nodded. He waited. She was thinking. At least she was not screaming bloody murder. Her hand again reached out, this time brushing his real hair.

"Your hair is as black and mysterious as deep space. Is that where you are from?"

He nodded.

She smiled. "That is good."

His warm relief was a sensation worth remembering for future reference when things might go bad.

They led her to the bridge, to a seat at the main console where both their languages could be immediately translated. The control room, particularly the holographic cube that held a three-dimensional transparent image of her home ship, had Vani enthralled. Sammy adjusted a microphone for her benefit, then leaned over and whispered in Eric's ear, "The Guard is holding them in a room, not questioning them. Strem has the impression they are about to be transferred."

"To where?" he whispered back.

Sammy shrugged. "Who knows. What are you going to tell her?"

"Everything." Eric bent over and slipped his green contacts out. He had not realized how irritating they were, nor had he known just how beautiful Vani was. Seen without the blur of the dye, her eyes were polished emeralds, her soft golden face a picture of all he had tried in vain throughout his adolescence to draw in his mind. Even Sammy appeared taken by her grace. The strangeness of his uncovered eyes did not appear to bother her at all.

"We are from another solar system," Eric said, simultaneously hearing the Kaulikan equivalent spoken over the bridge's speakers. "Our home world is hundreds of light years from here."

She touched the control console gently, the revelation obviously going deep inside her. She showed not a hint of disbelief. *"Did you come all that way in this tiny ship?"*

"Yes." He remembered his remark in the garden. "In the blink of an eye."

"Are there forests and mountains on your world?"

"Yes. And on millions of worlds in the galaxy."

Sammy looked worried at the direction the conversation was taking. Eric ignored him. His last words had started a bright hope burning in Vani; it was almost a tangible glow that could be seen without the aid of the opant coat. He was not going to let it go out.

"Why have you come to my people?"

"We passed too close to the nova. We lost our coolant. Our ship was in danger of exploding. We saw your fleet. We needed a source quick. That is why Strem and two others of our friends tried to take the coolant from your engineering department."

"But we would gladly have given it to you."

Eric shifted uncomfortably in his seat. "We are not supposed to be here. We were not sent here by our people. We felt it would be dangeous to reveal our true identities."

"We would not have harmed you."

Sammy spoke. "We were afraid, and still are, that you would be anxious to obtain our technology."

Vani's glow dimmed. *"You cannot help us?"*

"We want to," Eric said.

"But it is not our place to interfere with your people's destiny," Sammy added hastily.

"This ship can fly to the stars," she whispered to herself, shaking her head. It was like she was a condemned prisoner being shown a door out of jail, just before being told that the door was probably locked. *"Eric, you could take me to Lira? I could see it tomorrow?"*

Sammy answered before he could. "If our government would permit it."

Vani turned to Sammy. *"Would they?"*

"They haven't so far," Sammy said reluctantly. The answer contained its implications. A dark thought entered Vani's heart, as it had previously entered Eric's.

"Did your government know Kashi was going to be destroyed?"

"We're not sure," Eric said quietly.

"But with ships like this . . ." She gestured. She was no dummy. The strangers must have known. And done nothing. *"Why did you show me this ship, Eric?"*

"I guess I wanted to . . . ah . . . take you back to my world." It was a hell of a guess.

"Eric," Sammy began.

"Shh."

"And leave my people?" she asked.

He didn't answer, feeling ashamed.

She glanced at Sammy. *"It does not matter. I know it would not be allowed."* She stood. *"I should be going back."*

Eric jumped to his feet. "Oh, no, don't go!" He took her by the shoulders. "Vani, nothing is decided yet. Stay, give this a chance."

"But what can you do? What can I do?"

"The best we can. And unless we try, we'll never know what that might be."

"*But I take care of fruit trees. I know nothing important.*"

"To us, you're full of the unknown. Stay? Please?"

She looked out *Excalibur*'s windows, at the stars, wavering. "*My world now feels so small to have to return to.*"

"You've missed your study period, anyway."

She chuckled at the absurdity of his remark. "*Will you tell me more about the mountains?*"

"I'll show you movies of them. You'll stay?"

"*I will stay. For now.*"

"Good. We can fix that arm of yours in no time. Sammy, we have a Healer aboard, don't we?"

Sammy returned to his place at the helm. "Yes. But let's not forget some pressing business. Our friends are still being held captive."

"I haven't forgotten." He steered Vani back to her chair and leaned over Sammy's shoulder, reopening the implant channels. Three blinking orange dots inside the cube's model of Vani's ship represented his friends' position. "Strem, can you talk?"

("Yes," came the whispered response. "We're still in this damn room. There are two guards at the door. They've tied our hands behind our backs.")

"We're tracking you," Eric said. "You're in the second wheel. How are they treating you?"

("They haven't offered to feed us, but they haven't hurt us or anything. Okay, I suppose.")

"Why do you think you're to be transferred?"

("I heard the Kaulikans say the word. Hey, what's your rescue plan?")

"We're working on it. We've got the coolant."

("How did you manage that?")

"I *asked* for it. The Preeze Cap is cooling as we talk."

("Just don't leave without us," Cleo said, not sounding so hot.)

"Cleo? Jeanie? How are you two holding up?"

("I'm scared," Jeanie whispered. "Can you really get us out?")

Eric looked at Sammy, who shook his head. "We've got some good ideas," Eric said.

("You got that Kaulikan chick with you?" Cleo asked.)

"Vani is here," he said. "Stand by, I'll get back to you in a minute." He broke the connection. "Well?"

"It's fortunate we can at least speak to them. Do you really have a plan?"

"We'll send the Kaulikans a message. 'Release our people. We mean you no harm.' Send it now, in fact."

"And if they refuse?"

"We could bargain. They have something we want. We have something they want."

Sammy turned off the translator, leaving Vani in the dark. "We don't speak for The Union. We can't give the Kaulikans the details of the graviton or hyper drives."

"The Patrol doesn't speak for The Union either. Those coldhearted military creeps. . . ."

"We have to think of another way," Sammy interrupted.

"Like what? Hell!"

"What is it?"

He pointed out the forward window. A dozen bobbing lights were approaching *Excalibur*. Kaulikans on foot. His stunning the people at the air lock must have keyed the Guard to their position. A sensor beam on the console began to flash a warning. Sammy checked the readings.

"We've got a small craft above us," he said. "Rocket powered, slow and fragile."

"Can we bring the graviton drive up to power?" Eric asked.

"I was hoping to cool off for a while longer."

"With an angry mob outside?"

Sammy nodded, putting his hands to the controls. "I'll take us off into space."

"Wait! We should stay close."

"Why? I'll just take us out a million miles."

"No. I want to stay right on top of things." Eric had a reason why he didn't want to leave fluttering around the fringes of his subconscious, but it refused to come up to where he could grab it. Yet, he was sure it would be a mistake to dart off. "Put us in the tail of their ion drive. They won't be able to reach us there."

"We'll have to waste energy on our force field."

The individuals approaching up the dark alley were getting dangerously close. Eric had seen a film of someone getting caught in the force of a graviton flux being brought up to power. It had not been a pleasant sight. "Do it!" he ordered.

Excalibur began to hum as they lifted off the rotating wheel, the on-board gravity wavering slightly as the ship adjusted to the absence of the centripetal force. He watched the hand-held lights shrink beneath them as Vani's home fell away. But suddenly a brilliant searchlight swept the bridge. It was the craft their sensors had spotted. He could see the red flares of rockets through the glare, nothing else.

"There's another three approaching rapidly," Sammy said.

He threw his arm over his eyes, wincing. "Are they armed?"

"They appear to have lasers. I'm not sure what else."

"Close the window shields. Get us in the ion wake."

"They could throw atomics at us even there. I'd rather not have to mess with those."

"We must stay here. They'd be fools to try to destroy this vessel."

The external panels descended, cutting off the outside. Eric turned to the holographic cube in order to follow their movement away from the Kaulikan starship. The drone they had experienced on their initial approach to the fleet returned. But this time they were neither on the brink of collapse nor at the end of a mad deceleration, and *Excalibur* was able to handle the torrent of energy.

"I've got us out five miles from the tail of the ship," Sammy said a moment later. "Is that close enough for you? I don't want to strain our force field more than I have to."

"Yes. Can our sensors work through the turbulence?"

"Poorly. I can spot their small craft flitting around the fleet, but that's about all."

"Are they coming out to look us over?"

"No. We may have lost them, for the time being."

Eric reconnected the translator and went over to kneel by Vani's side. Throughout the commotion she had sat quietly, holding her sore arm. "We've moved a few miles away from your world, where we won't be disturbed."

She glanced at the ceiling. "*What is that strange sound?*"

"We're in the tail of your ion drive." Her eyes widened.

"Don't worry, it can't harm us."

"*All this power is at your command?*"

"If it were all mine, I would give it to you and your people."

"*I believe you.*" She touched the side of his face. "*Your eyes are much prettier without those silly lenses.*"

"They don't scare you?"

"*You did not scare the Sila. You do not scare me.*"

He looked at the floor. "You look much prettier without the lenses." He added hastily, "Though you looked fine to begin with."

She was amused. "*Now, I do not believe you.*"

"It is true; at least to someone from my world." He paused. "Vani, what I said a moment ago . . . I did not mean to expect you to leave your people. I was talking more in the way of you visiting my world."

She patted his arm. "*If your friends permit it, I would be happy to do so.*"

"My friends," he whispered, worried, glancing at the cube. The three orange dots were beginning to move. "Sammy, have you sent the message?"

"Just now. They told me to stand by. You know, what if they just turn off their drive? They could send out a hundred of those small craft and box us in."

"Can your people turn off their ion drive easily?" Eric asked Vani.

"*We shut it down twice a cycle. All of the worlds do so. But it takes much preparation beforehand.*"

"Here comes their reply," Sammy interrupted. "Someone named Rak—his title is First Councillor—wants to speak with the commander of our vessel."

"*Rak!*" Vani gasped.

"He's broadcasting from their flagship," Sammy said.

Eric vaguely remembered a Kaulikan in the corridor on the way to the cafeteria mentioning an inspirational speech Rak had given. He must be the big boss. Eric left Vani and took a seat beside Sammy. He was glad Rak would hear the computer and not himself. The computer would not sound nervous. Sammy nodded for him to go ahead.

"This is Eric, First Commander." He might as well give himself a title. "First, I would like to apologize for the unfortunate incident in the engineering department of one of your ships."

"We accept your apology," came the reply in the same mechanical voice as Vani's. *"Should you need supplies, coolant or otherwise, our every resource is at your disposal."*

"Thank you. We appreciate the offer. But what we really need is the return of our three crew members. We understand that you have them in your care?"

"That is correct. But as they do not speak our language, we have not been able to communicate with them to find out who they are."

Rak was civil enough but he had not addressed the issue.

"We are on an important mission, unconnected with your people. Our ship was momentarily overheated by the nova, and we required additional coolant. We mean you no harm and wish only to continue with our mission."

"Do you still need coolant?"

"No."

"Commander Eric, your people and your ship are a remarkable discovery for us. We would like to know more about you."

"We appreciate your curiosity. If you were to release our people, we would feel freer to talk."

"In time we will certainly free your people. But even though we accept your apology regarding their behavior, they have committed an act in Kaulikan territory in violation of Kaulikan law. They must be processed by the guidelines set down by that law." He added, *"Your cooperation could speed that processing."*

"What is the nature of the cooperation you desire?"

"Information about your people would be helpful, particularly as regards your intentions toward our fleet."

"I believe I have already addressed that point. We have no intentions toward your fleet. We just want our people back."

"Before their release, they must first be processed."

"First Councillor, were any of your engineering personnel actually harmed by my people?"

"All appear to be recovering nicely, including those who were knocked unconscious at the air lock near the resting place of your ship. We are, however, missing a young lady who was seen spending time in the company of someone who we now believe to have been one of your people. Her name is Vani AEG-172."

Vani looked both anxious and delighted that First Councillor Rak was concerned about her.

"She is here with us now and is doing well."

"May I ask, Commander Eric, if more of your people have infiltrated our fleet?"

"They have not," Eric said. Sammy was signaling him. "First Councillor, please stand by." He put him on hold.

"He's stalling," Sammy said. "He knows this ship didn't come from this solar system. He wants it, or at least, a look at it."

"Can you blame him?"

Sammy shrugged, checking the cube. Their friends were being moved toward the central shaft. "Better tell Strem what's happening."

Eric tapped in on the implants. "Strem, Cleo, Jeanie, we have the top man on the line. He's being stubborn. He wants information about us."

("Don't give it to him," Strem breathed.)

"We can see you're traveling. Do you know where to, yet?"

("No.")

Vani spoke up. *"Eric?"*

"A moment, Strem." Eric turned. "Yes?"

"Rak will want to see your friends in person."

"Will he come to them?"

"Rak has never left the flagship."

And his friends were being led to the axis, to free fall, exactly where a shuttle would depart from. "Vani, is transportation between the worlds of your fleet accomplished by small craft, like the one that flew by our window a few minutes ago?"

"Food ships are not so small."

"But when personnel travel from one world to another?"

Vani nodded. *"Then it is usually in the type of craft you saw."*

Eric felt a jolt of adrenaline. The solution was obvious, or else he was a genius. He reconnected the line to Rak. "First Councillor, I have come to a decision. I will wait till you are done processing my people and have released them. Please try to hurry. You may contact me when you are through. First Commander Eric out." He broke the connection before Rak could respond and returned to Strem. "You are as good as rescued. Cooperate with your guards. Stay loose."

("What are you going to do?")

"It will be a surprise." He turned off the mike.

"What *are* you going to do?" Sammy asked.

Eric stood and stretched. "We are going to clean out the cargo bay. Then when the shuttle leaves for the flagship, we are going to swoop in and swallow it up."

11

His plan sounded easier in theory than it turned out to be in practice. The first problem arose when Strem and the girls reached the central shaft and didn't go any further. Eric called to see what was happening, and when Strem answered—they were in another boring room, he said, doing nothing—his talking to Eric alerted the guards. Consequently, they were examined once again, and the implants were discovered and taken away. But initially, Sammy and Eric did not know this had happened, and when the three orange dots began to move back onto the second wheel, they figured their plan was ruined. When their next call to their friends, however, got them a baffled Kaulikan response, they realized the truth.

Then, to make matters worse, Rak and his people figured out where they were hiding *Excalibur* and sent out swarms of tiny ships to observe them. This was particularly troublesome because, with the interference from the ion wake, they were having a hard time confirming that no shuttle was leaving Vani's ship for the flagship; which was now their only way of keeping track of their friends, unreliable as it was.

Yet, Vani continued to insist Rak was the type of leader who would want to see personally what he was up against. Rak even called a couple more times, but Eric was short with him. "Until you release our people, there is nothing to discuss."

The one positive aspect of the delay was that Vani was able to put her arm under the Healer, which was capable of greatly stimulating the regrowth of bone. The noise and heat of the mechanism frightened her at first, but after an hour under its rays she was able to bend her wrist without pain. Brimming with excitement she gave Sammy and Eric appreciative hugs, using both arms.

Eric spent a portion of the wait washing the gold oil from his face and hands. When he returned to the bridge with his skin its usual light brown, Vani, to his dismay, acted horrified, cowering from him. But then she laughed at his pained expression. She was picking up their sense of humor fast. He hoped they weren't ruining her.

Finally, their sensors spotted a shuttle leaving Vani's world that was not heading toward *Excalibur*, but appeared to be making for the flagship.

"Prepare to dump the opant cartons in space," Eric said, following the movement of the shuttle in the cube. It was a thousand miles from Vani's world at the edge of the fleet to the flagship at the forward tip. They had tracked the shuttle over halfway before deciding upon its destination. The later they performed their rescue, the more confident they could feel that the tiny ship was indeed bringing their friends to Rak. Nothing was certain, however, and Eric knew if they didn't catch the right ship the first time, they wouldn't have another chance.

"I dislike using the graviton flux to sweep the clothes outside," Sammy said. "It's dangerous. We should have done it manually."

"Had we dumped the cargo already, it might have tipped them off to our plan." Eric was not worried about these minor technical difficulties. Something else was nagging at him, something he couldn't quite pinpoint. He had asked Sammy, what are we overlooking? Something we'll kick ourselves for if we fail, Sammy had replied.

Vani was not aware of any major weapon systems built into the fleet. But that did not mean they weren't there.

Vani tugged on Eric's arm. She had taken to touching him in small ways. Presumably, most Kaulikans, after reaching a certain point in friendship, were very affectionate. He was not complaining.

"*Are you throwing away all these beautiful jackets?*" Her opant coat, which she had removed for her sit under the Healer but otherwise wouldn't part with, was glowing a bright orange, which Eric assumed meant she was excited.

"Yes."

She looked unhappy. "*They are so pretty to waste.*"

Sammy agreed. "If Strem's uncle were here, he'd have something to say about this."

Eric chuckled. "He'd say, save the cargo and to hell with my nephew." Once more, he consulted the course of the shuttle in question still making a beeline for the flagship. "How much longer?"

"It will be there in five minutes. It's beginning to brake."

"All right. Drop the goods and let's go."

Excalibur shook, like the old freighter was coughing up its insides, which was not far from the truth. They rolled out of the ion wake and Sammy opened the windows, and they were able to see the trail of left-behind-opants ignite in the ion wake, turning to a cosmic ash. A number of the rocket-powered ships could be seen off their bow, multipronged flares scampering to keep up.

They didn't stand a chance. The hundreds of Kaulikan worlds stretched above and below and to the left for thousands of miles, purple candles on a circular slice of space. Then a bar of light pierced *Excalibur*'s holographic cube, representing the freighter's plotted course, and before the eye could blink, their relationship to the purple candles altered drastically. Vani practically fell over. Now they floated above the blue nine-wheeled flagship, staggering in its dimensions even after their experience with Vani's world, the remainder of the fleet trailing behind them like sparks on an infinitely receding cone. Bay doors were slowly opening atop the flagship's central shaft. And they sighted a shuttle, heading directly for those doors.

"*Such speed*," Vani gasped.

"Get in front of it," Eric ordered. "Force it to slow down."

Sammy maneuvered *Excalibur* between the shuttle and the flagship. To their immense surprise, the shuttle opened fire on them, pulses of bright red beams, which were soundlessly absorbed by their force field.

"Lasers," Sammy complained. "If we take them inside and they keep shooting, they could hurt us."

"We took them by surprise. Rak will order them to halt their fire. He doesn't want *Excalibur* damaged." And as if his voice had a power all its own, the lasers stopped. "See! Stay in front of them. Do you have our rear door open?"

"Yes." An alert began to sound on their sensor beams. "More ships are coming in from behind," Sammy muttered absently, concentrating on their approach to the shuttle.

"It doesn't matter. We'll have these guys in a moment." The Kaulikans were trying to squeeze past them, faking in every direction, but it was like a turtle trying to dodge a lion. *Excalibur* coasted to within a hundred yards, and Sammy elongated the graviton flux, the force field gripping the shuttle like an iron fist and holding it in one spot. The alert on their sensor beams grew louder.

"Hope they have the presence of mind to turn off their rockets," Eric said. The force field, compressing the exhaust, could cause the tiny ship to explode.

"Their pilot knows he's caught," Sammy replied, deftly manipulating the flux. The shuttle's rockets flickered out. "Not a moment too soon, with those other ones coming up on us."

"Yeah." Eric nodded. Then it hit him. Even before he whirled to check the report on the long-distance scanners, he remembered what he had been forgetting. They have been plotting and planning in their own little universe so long they had lost sight of the larger powers. The sensors confirmed his worst fears. The ships approaching at their rear were not small nearby rocket-propelled shuttles. They were large graviton-driven battle cruisers, millions of miles distant, but closing at speeds that would have left *Excalibur* standing still. "The Patrol!" he cried.

"*Who?*" Vani asked, worried.

Sammy consulted the scanner and his pale face turned a shade whiter. "There's two dozen of them," he whispered. "What a coincidence that they should show up now."

"It isn't a coincidence!" Eric yelled, furious with himself. All along, his subconscious had computed the danger. That is why he'd had a bad feeling about zooming out to a comfortable distance. A part of him had known they would be spotted immediately. "The Patrol has been looking for us all along. The interference we had on our communications earlier must have been caused by one of their tachyon sensors groping for us. And just now, when we raced across the fleet, the graviton wave we sent out must have made it a cinch for them to lock onto us."

Sammy nodded. "They probably figured out that we jumped beyond the web and have been tearing their hair out since, worrying that we'd run into the Kaulikans."

"Who is The Patrol?" Vani cried. The shuttle remained frozen in space only a few hundred yards away. They could actually see the frantic Kaulikan personnel through the shuttle's windows.

"Our government's armed forces," Sammy said.

"A bunch of military maniacs who sat by and watched Kashi get burned," Eric said bitterly.

"That's not fair. You don't know that for sure," said Sammy.

"Don't I? I tell you what's not fair! Last week this young lady standing here had to watch her brother go up in smoke!"

"The Patrol did not ignite the nova."

Eric chuckled. "I wouldn't be surprised if they did."

"Now you're being ridiculous. And what is the point of this endless argument? The Patrol is here and there's nothing we can do about it. Maybe it's a good thing."

"Right, they'll set everything straight," he muttered sarcastically, turning away from the window. Everything he had experienced in the last two days seemed to pour through him then, an avalanche of images that he only wished he could arrange into a coherent picture that would show him what to do: the initial broadcast they had received, the tape of Kashi's end, the walls melting, the parks in flames, the people running; the thousands of Kaulikans laboring over the ion drive, which could not compensate for its inefficiency with its size; Vani's face in the garden as she remembered Belri, her hand slipping through the sandy soil as she spoke of her future. All this talk of "racial destiny" versus "individual interference" had no strength next to the feeling he was left with. He looked at Vani. She was staring at him. Something in her eyes seemed to bring him to a decision. He stepped toward a supply cabinet located above the hyper drive.

"I'm going ahead and pulling the shuttle inside," Sammy said, watching him.

"Fine." Eric opened the cabinet and began to search. "How long till the cruisers arrive?"

"About a minute."

Outside the window the shuttle began to arc overhead, disappearing out of view behind the rear of the ship. A moment later there came a jolt as the force field deposited it inside their cargo bay, followed by a mild vibration—the cargo-bay doors closing.

"We have them," Sammy said. "I'm anxious to see if our friends are really inside."

"So am I." Eric found what he was looking for—a gun—and closed the cabinet.

"Are you going to try to get their guards to surrender?" Sammy asked, seeing the weapon in his hand.

"Not exactly."

"You know, I've been worrying about that. We've got

them trapped but they've still got Strem and Cleo and Jeanie trapped. "What should we do?"

"The unexpected." Eric raised the gun, pointed it at Sammy. "Move away from the controls, buddy."

"*Eric?*" Vani moaned.

Sammy seldom showed strong emotion. This was a classic exception. Pure unadulterated amazement filled his face. "What are you doing? This is ridiculous! We've got the others! We can leave!"

He took a step closer. "Put your hands up. Don't touch anything on the console."

Sammy stood slowly, backing away from his seat, his hands raised about as high as his belly button. "Why are you doing this?"

"I want a future for these people." Keeping an eye on Sammy, he expanded the image of the flagship in the cube, pinpointing the open bay doors, giving *Excalibur* a new destination. Their sensors had The Patrol cruisers perhaps thirty seconds away. In less time than that, the cruisers could snap them up in a tractor beam.

"You're going to take us inside the flagship!" Sammy gasped.

"Yes." He reached for the button to the graviton drive.

"No!" Sammy yelled, diving toward him. Eric saw him coming. He had the gun level and he had time to pull the trigger. But this wasn't some alien come to arrest him. This was . . . Sammy. He dropped the gun and tried to shove him away. Sammy was considerably weaker but every bit as quick, and as he fell backward onto the floor he grabbed Eric's arm and pulled him with him. The confrontation was not going to last. Eric could subdue him in seconds. The problem was he didn't have those seconds. Tangled on the floor in a knot of arms and legs, he glanced over at the screen and saw all two dozen of The Patrol cruisers entering the fringe of the Kaulikan fleet.

"Vani!" he shouted. "Push that large white button!"

Vani did not hesitate. She hit the button. The flagship did not merely rush toward them: one instant they were outside it, the next inside. But even here *Excalibur* began to wobble violently as the long invisible arm of The Patrol reached out to snap them back.

"Tractor beam!" Eric cursed, throwing Sammy aside and jumping back to the controls. The Kaulikan docking bay was huge, brightly lit, cluttered with small craft of a variety of designs and sizes. At a glance he saw several clear control booths crowded with watching people. But the wide bay door held his attention, obviously straining to close against the pressure of a projected graviton flux. Had there been atmosphere in the bay, no doubt he would have heard loud screeching. Twice the doors appeared to make a breakthrough, almost sealing, only to be pried apart by forces, though still distant, of a far higher magnitude. He began to manipulate *Excalibur*'s graviton flux, setting in motion a counterforce, a far weaker field but one having the advantage of proximity. The doors paused, suspended, trembling, then rifled shut. Vani let out a cry.

"*Eric!*"

The stun beam hit him between the shoulder blades. His mind registered the spot but he was unconscious before he reached the floor.

12

"I can't believe you shot me," Eric said, lying flat on his back and staring at the ceiling. He had awakened a couple of minutes before to Vani applying a damp towel to his forehead. She continued to kneel by his side, worried. He could probably sit up but was enjoying the "fallen hero" scenario. Besides, Sammy was standing over him, still holding the gun.

"I can't believe you pulled a gun on me," Sammy said.

"That is not as bad as actually going ahead and pulling the trigger."

"You started it."

"Are we still friends?"

Sammy glanced out the window, and Eric did likewise. A cluster of small craft had barricaded the closed bay doors. *Excalibur*'s position remained unchanged. "I don't know," Sammy said. "Now, *I'm* a hostage."

The situation had a certain ironic symmetry to it: the shuttle guards had Strem and the girls; they had the shuttle guards; the flagship had them; and The Patrol had the flagship. He realized their words were not being translated into Kaulikan for Vani's benefit. "You turned off the translator?"

"I don't want the two of you making plans behind my back."

"Sammy!"

"Oh, all right." He reactivated the bridge speakers.

"Does all this mean we will see Lira soon?" Vani asked.

He finally decided to sit up. He had a bump on his head, a strained muscle in his lower back, and an overall jangled nerve sensation that was an inevitable by-product of being stunned, but he would live awhile longer. "I'm working on it," he told her, patting her knee and climbing into a chair. "How long was I out?"

"Ten minutes. You snore."

"Have any Kaulikans come knocking on our door?"

"No, and none of them will," Sammy said, seriously. "I'm maintaining our force field. Eric, may I ask, what in the galaxy came over you?"

Eric winked at Vani. He felt better than he had in a long time. It was because he was doing the right thing, he was sure. "I guess I'm just a sucker for a pretty face."

"You've gotten us into a very dangerous situation."

"No more dangerous than when you popped us out of hyper space next to the nova." He sat up in his chair. "Would you put that gun away."

Sammy jammed it into his belt. "I think I'll keep it handy."

"Don't act so shocked. You saw it coming. And you know what I'm doing is right."

Sammy scratched his scraggly head. "What *are* you doing?"

Someone started to bang against the locked door at the end of the living quarters hallway that led to the cargo bay. "Have you had a chance to see who it is we picked up?" he asked.

"No, I was too busy trying to protect the ship from the outside, never mind the inside."

Sammy turned on the cargo bay's remote cameras. The shuttle rested in the center of the storage area, wisps of smoke rising from the tips of its hot rocket nozzles. Two armed Kaulikans—the guard uniforms were gray, not black, as he had supposed when he'd had his contacts in—were bent over the door, causing the noise. Sammy shifted the picture's angle and they peered straight through the shuttle's side windows. Sitting on the floor beneath a third Kaulikan guard, their hands and feet bound, were Strem, Cleo, and Jeanie.

"Not a bad plan, huh?" Eric asked.

"If we were somewhere out in space right now, I would agree with you. What are we going to do with these guards?"

"Nothing." He activated the cargo bay's speakers. "Hey, Strem, what did you think of the rescue?"

The Kaulikan guards looked up, anxious. Through the remote cameras they could see Strem smiling. "Not bad, not bad," he said, his voice coming by way of the open shuttle doors, low but clear. "Tell me, where did you stash the opants?"

Sammy and Eric exchanged looks. Vani burst out laughing. "I'm sure they were insured," Eric said.

Strem stopped smiling. "My uncle never insures anything! Where are they?"

"Cosmic dust," Eric said. "It was either you or them."

"Get us out of here," Cleo said. "I'm hungry."

"Cosmic dust," Strem moaned. "He'll kill me."

"Don't worry," Eric said. "He'll probably be in jail by the time we get home." He leaned over and whispered in Sammy's ear. "I would rather not tell him where we are."

"He has to know."

Eric sighed. More arguments. "I suppose."

"Do something about these goons," Strem said impatiently. "I have to go to the bathroom."

"I have some good news and some bad news," Eric began. "The Patrol has two dozen battle cruisers surrounding the Kaulikan flagship."

"Incredible," Strem said. "What's the good news?"

"We're locked inside the flagship," Sammy said.

"Is this some kind of joke?" Strem asked. "How did we get here? Eric, if you had anything to do with . . ."

A signal was coming in on the light-speed channel Rak had previously used. Eric immediately put Strem on hold. He was beginning to enjoy doing so. Kaulikan men and women in pressure suits were gathering outside, beyond the limits of *Excalibur*'s force field. He waved to them and a few waved back. He opened the channel to Rak. "First Councillor, this is Commander Eric. What's happening?"

Rak needed a moment to collect his thoughts. *"Commander, I was hoping you could clarify the situation. Are you aware that there are twenty-four alien craft surrounding our flagship?"*

"Yes. Have they tried to contact you yet?"

"No. Are these your people?"

"Yes."

"On their approach, they projected a force field of a nature similar to what envelopes your ship and tried to drag you out of our docking bay."

"We felt it."

"Why did you first capture our shuttle and then enter our flagship? These appear to me to be contradictory actions."

"We took your shuttle because we wanted our people back. We entered your flagship with the hope that you might have a chance to study our drive systems and learn how to reach the stars in hours rather than centuries."

"I'm thinking of shooting you again," Sammy said.

Rak was quick. *"That is an extraordinary offer. Do the individuals aboard the vessels surrounding our flagship share the same desire?"*

"I sort of doubt it," Eric muttered.

"You took this decision upon yourself. Why?"

"I like your people. I want to help them."

"We are gratified with your concern. Would it be possible for you to lower your defensive screen and allow us to board your ship?"

'That would be inadvisable at the moment."

"Have him tell his guards in our cargo bay to drop their guns," Sammy whispered.

"No," Eric whispered back. "If Strem gets to me now, he might beat me up."

"Commander, in your opinion, could the vessels surrounding the Kaulikan flagship be contemplating violence toward the Kaulikan fleet?"

"We are a civilized people. They will want to negotiate. Be patient. Wait till they contact you. I will talk to you when they do." He broke the line.

"I can't permit this," Sammy said, uneasily.

"You have no choice."

"You complained when Strem was giving orders. We all must have a say in this."

"Fine. It will change nothing."

Sammy related to the others exactly what had happened. Strem wasted no time in denouncing him.

"A cute alien smiles at you and you have to give away your own people's greatest secrets! We'll lose our tactical advantage. You think the galaxy's big, plenty of room for everybody, but that's not the way it is. They'll want some of the choicest planets. There'll be confrontations, maybe even a war, and it'll be all your fault!"

"Boy, Eric," Cleo added, "getting the opant coat free should have been good enough for any girl. Why did you have to give her the ship, too?"

"Sammy," Strem went on, "you're not handing over *Excalibur*. Turn our power to full. Ram us out of here.

"We would blow up," Sammy said.

"So what?" Strem retorted. "Better to die than to live and go down in history as cowards."

"I'm proud of you, Eric," Jeanie said. "Don't let them badger you."

"Thank you, Jeanie," he said, surprised at how much the remark meant to him. He was trying to play it cool but he was under intense pressure. It would have been nice to have the rest of his friends' support. Sensing his mood Vani came over and put her hands on the back of his shoulders, massaging his tight muscles.

"You feel all alone?"

"Yes. But I'm alone on top of a mountain. The view is excellent."

The Patrol's demand, blanketing every light-speed channel and worded in Basic Kaulikan, came a few minutes later.

"Release Excalibur, *or one by one, each half hour, a different Kaulikan vessel will be destroyed."*

13

The Patrol refused to return Rak's or Eric's calls. It seemed that until *Excalibur* was placed outside the flagship, they felt there was nothing to discuss. Eric had not expected them to react so strongly. He had thought that they would rant and rave and then eventually realize that they couldn't get *Excalibur* back, and be on their merry way. Maybe he was being naive, but he still thought the threat was only a bluff. He sat back in his chair after his latest talk with the First Councillor and checked the time: twenty-one minutes left until the deadline.

"Eric, you know how much I hate Mercury," Sammy said with a yawn, rubbing his bloodshot eyes. He had not slept in a very long time.

"They won't send you there. I'll take full responsibility." It went without saying that his noble offer would do Sammy no good if they all got killed. "Were you able to get through to any of the cruisers?"

"No. What did you tell Rak?"

He took a sip of the coffee Vani had brought him from

the galley. She had made it with at least two table-spoons of sugar. Since the demand had come in, she had been very quiet, no doubt waiting for her hero to unfold the next chapter in his marvelous plan. "That I have to meet with him in person," he said.

"But why? You can talk to him from here."

Eric set down his drink and stood and stretched. "He wants to see me. And I don't think he understands The Patrol's psychology or their military capabilities. He gave me the impression that the Kaulikan fleet was gearing up to resist an attack. I'm afraid he may even try to strike first. I have to talk to him face-to-face."

"And tell him what?"

"That The Patrol would never kill a hundred thousand innocent people."

"And what if they do?"

"I can't see that. Watching and doing nothing while Kashi was destroyed is one thing, but to take the initiative to murder people . . . they're barbarians but they've got *some* scruples. Rak is contacting the shuttle guards out back. They're leaving with Vani and me. They'll cause no trouble when we open the hallway door. Rak gave me his word, and Vani says a Kaulikan never breaks his word."

"What if the situation develops where *Excalibur* has to leave immediately? You could be left behind."

That possibility had passed through Eric's mind. His fantasies of being with Vani had always taken place with her in his world, not the other way around. With everything so up in the air, it would be ridiculous to worry about that now. On the other hand, it was a possibility that it might be wise to plan for. . . .

"I have to talk to Rak. No one else can."

"Your spring vacation might end up being a long one," Sammy said gloomily.

Eric slapped him on the side. "Don't worry. I was getting sick of school, anyway."

Muttering about foolish risks, Sammy equipped Eric with another implant and a portable translator the size of a fist that would allow him to talk to Rak directly. Neither of them mentioned aloud that he might have to rely upon the self-sufficient translator should it happen that the implant could no longer communicate with *Excalibur*'s computers.

Sammy did not trust Rak. Watching on the remote cameras he made sure the guards were at the far end of the cargo bay before he opened the hall door. He shut it as soon as they were through, and Eric didn't even have a chance to say a proper good-bye.

The Kaulikan guards had holstered their weapons and removed their hostages' binds. Jeanie and Cleo stood near the nose of the shuttle, looking no worse for wear. Strem was by the air lock, showing the guards how the pressure suits fit, obviously glad to be rid of them. Strem and the girls knew about The Patrol's ultimatum. They did not know about Eric's meeting with Rak.

"I have to go talk to the bigwigs now," Eric said, hugging Cleo and Jeanie together as Vani gave the girls a quick nod and a smile before heading for the air lock. "I'm sorry I got you both into this jam."

"You kept getting us out of jams," Jeanie said, following Vani with his eyes. "That girl is gorgeous. I'm glad you two got together."

Cleo was worried. "You'll be back soon?"

"Sure." But all of a sudden, Eric had this feeling he was lying. He thought of Cleo's crazy concerts that he had gone to, and the headaches they had given him, and of all the times he had watched Jeanie's dance routines, and the aches of a different kind her long legs had given him, and he felt a lonely tightness in his throat. Before it could spread and weaken his resolve, he hugged them again quickly, and strode away toward the air lock.

The guards were already dressed for the vacuum. Vani was halfway into her suit. He grabbed his own gear and began pulling it on.

"Where are you going?" Strem demanded.

"Rak is worried. I'm going to calm him down."

"Damn right he should be worried. You know who's probably out there, don't you? General Griffin."

Griffin was the top military commander in The Union. It had been his name at the bottom of the form rejection letter Eric had received in response to his application to the academy. Griffin's reputation could be summed up in one word: Strong.

"He might be," Eric said.

"So why are you leaving? After Griffin wastes one of their ships, they'll let us go."

"Aren't you glad to be getting rid of me?"

Strem never could hold a grudge. "I think what you did was dumb, but I can understand you doing what you thought was right." He started to look a bit worried. "No hard feelings?"

Eric smiled, reaching for his suit zipper. "None."

"Hey, why don't I go with you?"

"I doubt the Kaulikans would consider you a trustworthy adviser."

"Yeah, I guess not."

Vani surprised Strem by offering her hand. *"If someday you should visit my world again, I will show you all that you missed this time."*

The portable translator rested on the deck, turned off. Strem no longer had his implant. "What did she say?" he asked.

"That you are more handsome than any Kaulikan male in the entire fleet."

"Really?"

"Yeah, she likes your body."

Strem was impressed. "You're not a bad looker yourself," he said, pinching her cheek, causing the guards to laugh, and Vani to blush. "Have you ever thought of dying your hair?"

Vani nodded and smiled and quickly scooted into the air lock. Eric picked up the translator and his helmet and shook Strem's hand. "It's a long way from the spaceport in Baja, isn't it?"

"Maybe too long." Strem fidgeted. "Can't you just talk to him from the bridge?"

"The situation is too delicate for that."

"But Griffin's not going to back down."

"I think he will."

"I don't like this, Eric. I have this bad feeling."

He nodded. "So do I."

"Like we're not going to see each other again?"

"Yeah." But then he shook his head. "Strem, we got through The Tachyon Web, survived the nova, and snuck inside an alien ship. Hell, I'll see you again. Like you said, the galaxy's not that big."

They said good-bye. The deadline was fifteen minutes away.

The addition of color made his reentry into the Kaulikan community a new experience. Without his contacts, the abstract mosaics on every other wall took on a new richness. They floated away from *Excalibur* past a blaze of millions of carefully fitted tiles that subtly but nevertheless powerfully portrayed a universe caught in a conflict of bright and dark forces. He carried

the image into the elevator that led them out of the
vacuum and the free fall. Doubts pricked his conscience.
Which side would the future place him on in this conflict?

Bodily weight and fresh honey air returned. They
removed their helmets and exited onto another one of
the Kaulikans' long corridors. The shuttle guards left for
duties unknown while two women in blue suits appeared for Vani and Eric. They were taken to an elabo-
rate control center that impressed Eric as a war room.
It was dominated by four large screens set before rows
of manned computer boards. A hundred uniformed people were present and half of them were in motion. A
tense chatter congested the air. The situation was clear:
Emergency. The large screens alternated different views
of The Patrol's battle cruisers, sleek and cold, shining
with the reflected light of the distant nova, confidently
arranged in a tight formation. Plus, there were flashes
of the preparations being made inside various Kaulikan
ships: slow, cumbersome missiles being loaded, primitive beam weapons being aimed. He had to get Rak's
finger off the trigger.

Their escorts led them to an elevated room at the
rear of the control center through whose glass walls the
hive of activity could be overseen. Here there was a
surprising lack of equipment, only a single computer
screen and keyboard set near the head of an oval table
around which four Kaulikans were seated: two men
and two women, all dressed in silky white gowns that
reminded Eric of ancient Roman senators.

The man at the head of the table stood and the others
followed his example. He was taller than any Kaulikan
Eric had seen, younger than his fellow Councillors, and
marked from them by a bright blue sash tied around his
waist. His face lacked his race's usual softness, yet it
was not a hard face, rather one whose warmth had been

molded through years of painful choices to something closer to wisdom. Vani trembled visibly with awe.

"*Rak*," she whispered.

The First Councillor raised his palm toward Eric, then toward himself, welcoming him. Their escorts pulled up two chairs. Rak indicated Eric should take the one closest to himself. Eric set the translator on the table and turned it on. He sat down, glancing at Vani, who was keeping her eyes downcast.

"*I appreciate you leaving your ship to come and speak with us,*" Rak said. The translator gave Eric the English in the neutral mechanical voice. Still, he was struck by how much deeper Rak's actual words were than his fellowmen's. He could have been an Earthman. "*I trust this device you have brought will allow us to communicate easily?*"

"Yes."

"*We have nine minutes till your Patrol's deadline. As you know, they refuse to speak with me, except to say that when your ship is placed outside ours, they will withdraw. You understand why I am reluctant to comply with their demand?*"

"Yes."

"*Word of the capabilities of your ship has spread throughout our fleet. This is unfortunate because it has given my people a hope that is now difficult to take away. Had the rumor of your remarkable propulsion systems not spread, I would comply with the demand rather than risk this danger. As it is, I am undecided. I tell you this so you will have a clear grasp of our situation before offering advice.*"

"I understand," Eric said. The eyes of the four High Councillors were on him, and behind them he could feel the heartbeats of the millions of Kaulikans spread throughout the fleet. The memory of the end of Kashi gave him the nerve to speak persuasively. "I say do nothing. My people's armed forces will not purposely kill your people. Their threat is an idle one."

Rak listened to the translation, all the while studying him. "*Are you sure of this?*"

"I cannot be sure."

"*Your Patrol's vessels are small compared to ours. Should their demand be genuine, do they possess the power to destroy one of our ships?*"

"Most definitely."

Rak glanced to the other Councillors. One of them, an elderly lady with pale green eyes and a high birdlike voice, spoke. "*Commander Eric, we are a peaceful race, but in the construction of our fleet we did give some thought to defense. Your Patrol has only twenty-four ships present. They have threatened us with violence. This Council has considered the possibility of destroying them before they have an opportunity to try to carry out their threat.*"

"That is out of the question. I have seen the limits of your technology. Your antimatter missiles, your lasers, they would be like smoke against the screens of The Patrol cruisers. Besides, there are more than two dozen ships in this vicinity. I estimate there are over a hundred."

The old lady was skeptical. "*We have no evidence of their presence.*"

"They are probably observing from a distance. But they could, if they wished, enter your fleet and be invisible to you. They possess sophisticated cloaking devices. Not that more is necessary. One Patrol cruiser alone could destroy every ship in this fleet in a matter of seconds."

"*Yet you maintain that we should not give in to their demand?*" Rak said.

"I emphasize their strength so you will discard any idea of using violence against them, before or after the deadline."

The old lady was unconvinced. *"How can we be sure you are not trying to manipulate our decision for the benefit of your Patrol?"*

"He is not," Vani said.

"Child," the old woman began.

"Let her speak," Rak interrupted. He turned to the young girl who had lifted her head from its humble position. *"You are Vani?"*

"Yes, my Councillor. I have been with Eric. He knows our sorrow over Kashi and over the length of time we must spend in space before reaching Lira. He has striven against the desires of his closest friends to try to help us."

Rak considered for a moment. *"Eric, you are young to command a ship. Is that not unusual with your people?"*

He debated telling him he was much older than he looked but he suspected Rak would know he was lying. "I am not really a commander. A few of my friends and I, we borrowed the ship in your docking bay. We're . . . ah . . . on vacation."

A stir went through the Councillors, except for Rak, who smiled faintly. *"I regret that my people are no longer allowed vacations to far-off places."* He paused, said seriously, *"Our time is almost gone. I waver. You ask me to risk a great deal."*

At that instant Eric almost backed down. Rak's last words cut deep. These were *his* people that were being gambled. He looked to Vani. She could practically read his mind.

"I am not the only one who wants to walk in a real forest," she said.

Eric cleared his throat. "First Councillor, do you know for a fact that Lira has inhabitable planets circling it?"

"The star has planets, two approximately the size of Kashi. But we do not know if we can live on either of them."

"And if you can't, will your descendants have the fuel to go elsewhere?"

Rak saw his point. He came to a decision. *"We will wait."*

Exactly thirty minutes after issuing its demand, The Patrol vaporized one of the Kaulikan ships.

14

The shuttle belonged to The Patrol. They had sent it over empty. They didn't want any Kaulikan craft entering their battle cruisers. Eric knew how to pilot it but wasn't given an opportunity to display his skills. The moment he cleared the flagship bay doors, with Rak as his only passenger, The Patrol locked onto them with a tractor beam. Perhaps there was a subliminal message in the action: we are the power here, not you. Then again, The Patrol had already made their message painfully clear.

Eric peered through the shuttle window toward the remains of the Kaulikan vessel, a faintly glowing red smudge against the black of space. He shuddered at the memory of the screens in the flagship war room switching suddenly to the imploding ball of energy. The cry of anguish bursting from those present had almost sent him into a swoon. He might have given up right then and there had he not known that things could get much worse. With the exception of Rak, the Councillors had immediately shouted for retaliation. It had been Eric's task, fighting his radically tarnished credibility, to convince them that they would lose a hundred ships as quickly as they had lost the first one if they so much as fired a single missile. Rak had listened to him. Speaking to the frantic control center without the aid of a PA, he had managed to restore a semblance of calm. Then the good news, if it could be called that, came through. The target had been one of the fleet's ten fully automated factory vessels. No one had been killed.

The Patrol had made their point. They weren't bluffing. Again Rak had sent a message requesting a meeting. This time it was accepted. The Patrol was obviously willing to sit down and negotiate as long as the other party was convinced that the gun being held to their heads was loaded. The reply also contained a stipulation. The Patrol wanted—not "wanted to see" or "wanted to talk to" just "wanted"—the captain of *Excalibur*. The individual sending the reply had been General Griffin.

Hearing the fearsome name, Eric had barely had the presence of mind to scribble out the sequence of notes to give to Vani that would hopefully find their way to Strem, should he be unable to talk to him again. Before leaving, he had made sure she would be allowed to remain in the Councillors' room while Rak and he were with Griffin. He had not known until then that Kaulikans could cry. She had not believed he would return. She was a smart girl.

"*Do you know this General Griffin?*" Rak asked, sitting beside him in the ten-seater shuttle, looking remarkably calm.

"I know of him. He is occasionally interviewed on our news network. He is a cunning man. He has always impressed me as someone who was capable of doing anything to reach a set objective."

"*Is he a truthful man?*"

"He won't have any need to lie to you," he answered with a trace of sarcasm.

Rak was regarding him curiously. "*You are blaming yourself for the destruction of the factory?*"

"I gave you bad advice."

"*That has yet to be seen. One thing you have tried to do was give us something we desperately need. For that alone, I owe you a great thanks.*" Rak's eyes strayed to the nova.

Since the time they had jumped outside the web it had begun to fade slightly, the shells of plasma cooling toward the lower end of the spectrum.

The two of them were of separate origins, together in the middle of nowhere, and yet, for a moment, they shared the same thought. Rak spoke it aloud. "*Soon it will burn less bright than it has in billions of years. Our grandchildren will have trouble finding it in the sky. I wish, if we are to be given this chance that you bring, that it could have been a year ago, or even a day before the nova. Then, at least, those left behind on Kashi could have known that we would be safe.*"

"The nova was what allowed me and my friends to sneak past The Patrol's security screen, what we call The Tachyon Web." Eric glanced toward the growing silver cluster of battle cruisers looming in the midnight like icy needles waiting to impale them. "When I think about it, I see that the web must have been built because of your people, to keep a stray trader from finding and helping your world." Concern had driven him into his predicament, but also bitterness, and it was the latter that he tasted in his mouth. "I'm sorry I was late."

Even with his words going through the translator, Rak was sensitive to his tone. "*Third Councillor Maga told you we are a peaceful people and this is true. But it was not always so. I have the sense that our race is much older than yours. We spent many of our early years, too many, fighting amongst ourselves. Sometimes I have thought that our sun, watching from its place in the sky, grew tired of our foolishness, of the many chances we did not take, and decided enough was enough. And then when we started to live as we should, when the light of our sun began to change and deepen our shadows, it was too late."* He took Eric's hand and pressed it between his. Like Vani's, his touch was warm and soft. *"Son, you can help us without hating them."*

Eric shook his head. "They saw the nova coming. They did nothing."

"Had we come together as a people sooner, we would have had time to develop ships as strong and fast as your Patrol's. What we have suffered as a people, it was our own doing."

"I can't see how that makes them any less guilty."

Rak let go of his hand. *"We will be there soon. Is there anything you wish to tell me now, anything that I could do for you?"*

"Yes. Whatever is decided, when the time comes for you to return to the flagship, ask to speak into that room where we left Vani. Make sure that I am by your side."

Eric saw no one during his first hour aboard the battle cruiser. Immediately upon being taken inside, the shuttle opened on both sides, and Rak and he were ordered by a young indifferent male voice to exit in opposite directions. At that point he tried to call Strem and Sammy, using his implant. He had spoken to them via the communicator just before leaving the flagship and had wanted to see them again, but Griffin was not one to be kept waiting.

Eric had told them of the vaporized factory ship, and Strem had sounded uncharacteristically upset at the news. Or maybe it had been the fact that Griffin had specifically demanded to see his best friend. Neither Strem nor Sammy had been able to offer any advice. And now, Eric was not surprised to find that his implant signal was being jammed.

The young indifferent male voice spoke again. "Remove all equipment from your person." That was just the beginning. He was directed to a decontamination chamber where he had to strip naked and sit for ages in a chemical-smelling steam under a glaring purification beam that swelled his sinuses and made his entire body itch. If they were trying to cut him down to size before they stepped on him, they were doing an excellent job. It annoyed him even more than they were undoubtedly doing the same or worse to Rak.

The voice finally permitted him to leave the chamber. He was blow-dried in an adjoining room and he found a bland green shirt and pair of pants waiting on a hanger. Once dressed, two expressionless ensigns appeared, smartly attired in the standard black and orange-lined Patrol uniforms; the fleet emblem, a single descending white triangle dotted in the center with an orange star, was pinned to their left breasts. Neither had their pistols drawn but Eric received the distinct impression that they would whip them out if he so much as coughed. They marched him into a small elevator and then down a narrow hall. The air was clean but lifeless, and he longed for the fragrances of Vani's garden.

They came to a stop outside a closed metal door. A

button was pushed. A gruff voice responded. "Send him in and then get the Kaulikan."

The door opened and Eric stepped forward into a personnel quarters that was sliced in half by a floor-to-ceiling black grill, a bed on one side, a desk fitted with a holographic globe on the other. The trimmings were sparse: a couple of plants, a shelf packed with old-fashioned *paper* books, a family portrait hanging on one wall. But there was a decoration of note—a large intricate wooden model of a sixteenth century naval vessel rested atop a cabinet. Eric knew his history; it was a representative of the Spanish Armada that bad weather and a swifter English Navy had crushed. He was surprised that Griffin would have a loser in his own room.

"Have a seat," General Griffin said without looking at him. The Commander was shorter than he appeared on news programs, stockier, his heavy face hard and lined, sitting atop thick shoulders with nary an inch of neck showing. His thinning hair was cut short, silver bristles, and he was a far from handsome man. Most would have quietly thought him ugly. Yet he reminded Eric of Rak. Each had an innate aura of authority about him. Eric sat down and waited.

Griffin was sitting behind the desk, studying the personnel file of Eric T. Tirel as if the actual article were not present. His blunt fingers and flat black eyes sped through the early years, finally halting on what must have been a relevant note. Then Griffin looked at him, his expression impassive, impossible to read. "You applied to the academy and were rejected," he said.

Eric kept his voice even. "Yes, sir."

So much for his personal history. Griffin turned off the globe. He wsan't going to tell him why he had been rejected.

"Have you zeroed out *Excalibur*'s computers?"

"No, sir."

"Have you melted down its graviton drive?"

"No, sir."

"Have you sabotaged its hyper drive?"

"No, sir."

Griffin leaned forward, his uniform stiff and tight, clasping his stubby hands atop the desktop. He was not a young man, Eric thought, but he looked like he had the strength to throttle a teenage traitor. "You are saying in effect that the Kaulikans are in possession of a fully operational starship?"

"Yes, sir."

Griffin took a breath, narrowed his gaze. "Why are you here, Tirel? We expected Strem Hark or Sammy Balan. Checking backwards, we have determined that it was originally their idea to penetrate the web."

"None of my friends wanted to give *Excalibur* to the Kaulikans. It was entirely my idea."

"Did they try to stop you?"

"Yes. But I was holding a gun." He added, "I gave the Kaulikans the ship not because I was rejected by the academy, but because I wanted to help them." Griffin was not impressed. Eric felt anger on top of his fear. "Don't you want to help them, sir?"

A light blinked beside the globe. "Yes?" Griffin said.

"We have the First Councillor, sir," an ensign outside the door said.

Griffin stood. "Send him in."

Eric also stood. "I guess I'll wait outside."

"You'll stay," Griffin said, straightening his uniform.

Rak strode into the room, the door closing behind him. He presented his palm to the General and then to himself in the traditional Kaulikan greeting. To Eric's surprise Griffin imitated the gesture perfectly, something that should have required practice. Then the General stepped forward and offered his hand. Rak shook it firmly. And it was true—the two were from different primordial seas, but they had something in common that went deeper than appearance or manner. They were both powerful individuals. Nevertheless, the comparison did not improve Eric's appreciation of Griffin. There were no two ways about it—the man was responsible for genocide.

Griffin activated a translator and offered Rak a chair. Eric took his seat without waiting for permission.

"This is a secure room," Griffin began. "This conversation is not being overheard by anyone else aboard this ship, or by anyone in any of the other ships under my command. This conversation is not being taped. All that is said in this room, can stay in this room." He paused. "First Councillor, I take it none of your people were killed or injured in the destruction of your automated ship?"

"*Nobody was physically hurt.*"

"Is it now clear to you that your fleet could not successfully engage in a battle with our fleet?"

"*It was clear to me before you destroyed our factory.*"

"We did not act without provocation. You are refusing to return property that does not belong to you."

"*Excalibur* does not belong to The Patrol," Eric interrupted.

"*Excalibur* is bound by laws that The Patrol has been designated to enforce," Griffin responded, showing no obvious annoyance at being contradicted, showing no real emotion at all.

"*We have laws, too,*" Rak said. "*You violate many of them with your attack and your threats.*"

"I have no choice. We do not want to harm your people," Griffin said. "If you will return *Excalibur* immediately, we will allow your fleet to continue unobstructed."

"*Whether you intended to or not, you have already harmed my people, in ways that cannot be measured by bodily damage alone.*"

"You demoralized them," Eric said bitterly.

Griffin ignored him. "First Councillor, ours is a democratic society. Our people, on all our worlds, are allowed to elect their leaders. These leaders create the laws we are to live by and in turn choose people such as myself to make sure these laws are never broken. To follow the will of my people I must obey the orders of my superiors. And they have stated, within the last couple of hours, that under no conditions is your fleet to be allowed access to *Excalibur*. If you do not comply with our request and return *Excalibur*, I have been given authority to take whatever steps are necessary to prevent you from taking advantage of our technological developments."

Eric fumed. "Our people would never do this to the Kaulikans. The men who gave you that order are out of touch with the masses of The Union."

"*I speak for my people,*" Rak said quietly. "*They know that with* Excalibur *the stars are within reach. They have recently lost everything. They have suffered terribly. But now, though the destruction of the factory has struck fear into their hearts, they have hope. General Griffin, I cannot give you back the ship.*"

The lines had been drawn. They were sharp. Neither side would step over to the other side. Not unless they were pushed. Griffin turned on his desktop holographic globe. In the center of the black crystal gleamed the Kaulikan flagship. His face turned grim. "Then you leave me with no choice."

"*I have no choice.*"

"Your people would rather die?"

"Than give up this chance? Yes."

"What will you do to them?" Eric whispered.

Griffin was blunt. "The flagship will be destroyed."

"No!" Eric breathed. "There are hundreds of thousands of people aboard it!"

The General pushed a button on his desk. "This is Griffin. Has target been programmed into matrix disrupters?"

"Programmed. Status yellow and waiting, General."

"Go to status red. Define target's matrix within our fields."

Eric's fear and anger skipped a cold beat as a painful sense of unreality tightened his chest, clotting his heart's blood. He had been so caught up in the tragic size of the confrontation and the years he might have to spend on Mercury working sixteen hours a day under nauseous conditions that his mind had played a trick on him and he had momentarily forgotten the impact the situation could have on his friends. Sammy . . . Strem . . . Vani . . . they were all on the flagship! And this *creature* of a man was going to turn them into rarified plasma.

And it would be *all* Eric Tirel's fault.

"Disruption is defined."

"Prepare to disrupt." Griffin looked at Rak. "Place *Excalibur* outside the flagship. Now."

Rak was studying Griffin with an intentness that was somehow disconnected from the crisis, as if there were no hundred of thousands to worry about, no deadly armada surrounding all that was important to him; there was only Griffin's face, something in it that fascinated the First Councillor. Rak did not answer.

"Awaiting final command, General?"

"Countdown disrupt matrix, thirty seconds."

"Thirty . . . Twenty-nine . . . Twenty-eight . . ."

Eric looked back and forth, from one to the other, his head grinding on his neck, his muscles tightening into hard lumps. This could not happen, he told himself, he could not let it happen.

"You understand what we are going to do?" Griffin asked.

Rak was hardly listening. *"I understand."*

"You'll gain nothing," Griffin said.

Rak nodded slightly, holding the General's eyes; or rather held *by* them. *"We will both lose."*

"Twenty . . . Nineteen . . . Eighteen . . ."

Eric exploded. He leapt to his feet, his chair toppling over at his back, terror and rage combining in a fearsome possession. He reached across the desk, grabbing Griffin by the collar, feeling the weight of the General in his trembling hands as he tried to pull the man from his seat.

"You animal!" he cursed. "You sit here and tell us of your orders and you give your orders and all those people out there are going to die and you're going to die, too, 'cause I'm going to rip out your filthy fat throat!"

Griffin glanced at him with mild distaste. "Sit down, Tirel, and shut up."

"I'll kill you," Eric swore, nevertheless feeling his supposed deathgrip loosening. Rak touched his side.

"Son," he said gently.

"But my friends," Eric moaned, letting go of the General, his eyes watering. As hot as it had burned, as quickly it burned out, and as his wrath died, he was left feeling cold and weak. He no longer cared about what had happened to Kashi, or what would happen to the rest of the Kaulikans. He just wanted his friends to live. He turned to Rak, pleaded. "Give him the ship. Please?"

Rak stood and put his arm around him, placing his lips near his ear and whispering words that it was remarkable the translator was able to catch, words Eric did not understand. *"He does not want it."*

"Nine . . . Eight . . ."

The pressure was smothering. Eric could hardly speak. "What does he want?"

"To know what is best."

"Five . . . Four . . ."

Rak turned to Griffin. *"You knew me before I walked in. You do not need to play this game."*

"Hold fire," Griffin said into the microphone beside the globe. "Return to status yellow. Await my command."

"Status yellow and waiting."

Griffin erased the flagship in the globe and stood from his place behind the desk. He was deep in thought, the lines in his face now set with weariness rather than cruelty. Or had his expression really changed? Eric no longer knew what he was seeing because he no longer knew what he was looking for. He collapsed in his chair, limp with exhaustion while Griffin stepped to the model of the Spanish warship, placing his back to them, touching the main sail, a yellow mast that could have been sewn by hand. A full minute went by in silence.

"First Councillor," Griffin said finally, not looking at them. "On Kashi, before the change in your sun, you had oceans like those on our home world."

"Yes. And we had primitive vessels similar to your model."

The General fingered the ship's tiny steering wheel. "My people's planet is called Earth. And in my home on Earth I used to keep many models such as this one, of old sailing vessels. I used to build them; it was a hobby of mine. Even as I rose through our service and began to command ships of extraordinary power, I retained a fascination for such craft. Slow and fragile, at the mercy of the elements, they demanded a great deal from a commander. But aboard a ship like we're in now, nothing is left to chance. Everything is calculated and computed, and is perfect. Occasionally, I think, I would envy those old captains, their strength in the face of unknown dangers." He stopped, then added, reluctantly, "But I don't anymore."

They waited for the General to continue. He did not, lost in some personal reverie.

Rak had to ask, "*Something happened to change your mind?*"

Griffin plucked a small wooden chip from inside the model and returned to the desk, taking his seat. He loosened his collar and leaned back, glancing to the wall where his family portrait hung, a large oil of himself and his wife—a short, elegant blond-haired lady—and three smiling teenage children.

"Yes," Griffin said, his voice less gruff. "Several years ago I took a sailing expedition from a group of islands we call the Philippines to a continent named Australia. My hobby had taken on a serious note and I had had constructed a forty-foot wind-driven ship that I had the bad sense to believe I could steer across a thousand miles of ocean. I practiced with the ship and its sails on a number of short excursions, then set off on the big adventure without a communicator or mechanical propellor of any type. I had my son with me."

Eric remembered the incident. It had been in the news, a famous tragedy. He did not understand Griffin's purpose in narrating it to the leader of a people he was essentially at war with.

"On Earth," Griffin continued, "we have a reliable weather forecast network. I would like to say that it failed on this occasion and that is why my expediti͏ turned into a disaster. But I knew of the impending storm before I left the Philippines. We were underway three days when it hit. By the standards of earlier mariners, it was not particularly fierce. But I was inexperienced. The ship would not respond at the push of a button as would a Patrol cruiser. We took on a great deal of water. Mark was bailing it out. A wave came. He was washed overboard. It was a small miracle I survived. We never found his body."

Griffin sat up straight, resting a hand on the desk, the chip he had taken from the model resting beneath his stubby fingers. "Suffice it to say, I lost my enthusiasm for primitive ships. Now I never give Nature a chance, on Earth or in space. I'm sure you can understand that, First Councillor.

"You were right, I did know you before you walked in. I have watched you from afar for many years. Though it was obvious to us, it wasn't clear to your scientists till near the end that your sun would nova." A note of admiration entered his voice. "But you pressed for your fleet to leave when it did, even though a delay would have allowed for the construction of more ships and room for more people. You didn't trust your sun and you were right not to."

Eric remembered Vani's reference in the garden to Rak, how he, too, had left family behind. Eric realized that Griffin knew of the First Councillor's sacrifice. Yet he had no idea what the General was driving at. Rak was quicker.

"*You see my fleet as being at the mercy of the elements, like your sailing boat?*"

"Yes. Your fleet is slow and vulnerable. But it is also ¬d beautiful. I have patrolled this corner of The Web for twenty years. I watched as you built your ships, and put everything you had into them. I admired you. It was a mighty labor."

Rak nodded. *"It still is."*

Griffin opened a drawer in his desk and removed a black, cube-shaped device, about a foot in diameter with a glass viewplate on one side and a slit at the top. "Do you recognize this?" he asked Rak.

"It looks similar to our instructors."

"It is a working replica of one of your instructors. We are able to directly scan your computers' data banks. That is how I obtained the specifics of its design. I had a technician on Earth, not in the service of The Patrol, put it together."

"Why?" Eric asked, still waiting for the light to dawn.

"To see how well this could be read by an instructor." Griffin held up the chip. It was not made of wood, but of silicon. It was an old-fashioned computer chip.

"What the hell?" Eric muttered.

Griffin dropped the chip in the top slit of the instructor and pushed a side switch. The viewplate glowed. He handed it to Rak. The First Councillor studied it for a moment.

"This is a translation of your language into ours?"

"The dictionary is a necessary preface. Fast forward the material and have this young man look at it."

Rak did as requested. Eric peered into the viewplate. Technical schematics and lengthy explantory pages flowed by: Dr. Pernel's gravity flux theories; Dr. Preeze's papers on hyper link; Dr. Hial's notes on interspacial navigation . . . Eric lowered the instructor, almost dropping it on the floor. Griffin reached across the desk and took it from him, removing the chip.

"What is it?" Rak asked, even though he seemed to know.

"Instructions on how to build the graviton and hyper drives," Eric heard himself say.

"*Detailed* instructions," Griffin corrected. "As I watched you through the years, I used to think, if I had the chance, what would I tell you?" He tapped the chip. "This has everything." He handed it to Rak. The First Councillor slipped it in a pocket beneath the folds of his gown. He was not surprised, but still deeply touched.

"*Thank you.*"

"But why did you wait till now to give him this information?" Eric asked. He could not assimilate what had just happened. That General Griffin was a blood-thirsty maniac was deeply engrained in his psyche. There had to be a catch. "Why did you wait till after Kashi was destroyed?"

"I had my orders. I have never disobeyed an order." He stopped. "I see that you are not satisfied with that answer. Neither was I. But I understood my superiors' reasoning. They are not the heartless savages you imagine, Tirel. They are just . . . cautious people. They wanted to wait and see." Griffin closed his eyes briefly, showing the first real signs of emotion, glimpses of a disturbing realization. "Then the sun exploded, and *I* saw more than I wanted to. Still . . . I continued to wait."

"For what?" Eric asked.

"Maybe for you, Tirel, some excuse."

"But that whole show about destroying the flagship?"

"*A final test,*" Rak said.

Griffin nodded. "I still had my doubts. But your resolve, First Councillor . . . that erased them. Return *Excalibur* to us, then build your star drives in secret. Outfit every ship in your fleet. And when the day comes when your people suddenly jump out of our observable reach, I will feel somewhat forgiven for having waited, and for having needed an excuse."

Rak's quick insight hit again. *"But on that day, your superiors will know what went on in this room?"*

Griffin shrugged. "So they will. So what?"

"You'll be up for high treason," Eric said, impressed.

"That won't be as bad as being caught in a storm."

Griffin did not need to glance at the picture of his son. Rak and Eric understood.

The meeting was over. They stood and shook hands. Eric felt like dancing with joy and would have if he hadn't been so limp with relief. And if not for one other small detail. . . .

"What's going to happen to me?" he asked.

The General was still a hard man. "You know too much, Tirel. If word leaked out of what went on here, before the Kaulikans could build their drives, I could not guarantee what action The Patrol would take."

"I won't tell anybody. None of my friends will either."

"None of your friends will know what's happened. First Councillor, have I your word that *Excalibur* will be placed outside in space before Tirel and you can return to the flagshsip?"

"Yes."

Eric was aghast. "Are you saying I can't go home?"

"You can't," Griffin said.

Rak touched his arm. *"We will take care of you, son. We owe you so much."*

He felt profoundly sad, ready to cry, and had to struggle to keep back the tears. No more clowning with Strem and Sammy. No more shark hunts off the coast of Baja. No more mountain climbing . . . "But my parents," he stuttered. "You can't just tell them I died."

"I will meet with them personally," Griffin promised.

"They will be told you're on a special assignment for The Patrol."

"But when I don't come home . . ."

"They will know that you are safe. I will see to it."

Eric sniffed, then tried to hide it by chuckling. "But I don't even speak Kaulikan."

"You may keep the translator in the shuttle."

Rak squeezed his arm. *"We were a happy people once, and will be again soon. I believe you will find happiness with us."*

"I was never really that happy on Earth," he admitted. He looked Griffin in the eye. "All right, I'll go. But what about my friends?"

"They'll think the First Councillor surrendered *Excalibur.*"

"Will they be punished?"

Griffin shook his head. "All of you youngsters helped me make this difficult decision. I have influence, for now. They will be fine."

"When the Kaulikans make their first hyper jumps, will The Tachyon Web come down?"

Griffin raised a silver eyebrow. "You are clever, Tirel. It's a shame the academy rejected you."

"Why *did* they reject me?"

"You sent in your application late."

"Is that the only reason?"

"Yes." He added, "The web will probably come down, in time."

"Would it be possible to say good-bye to my friends?"

"No."

"How about just over a communication beam?"

"I can't chance what you might tell them."

Rak let go of Eric's arm. *"General, may I speak to my fellow Councillors to tell them to prepare to release Excalibur?"*

"Of course." Griffin adjusted a dial next to the empty globe. "That is the same channel we spoke on earlier?"

"*Yes.*"

Griffin pointed Rak toward the microphone. "Go ahead, First Councillor."

Rak leaned over the desk and told his people that the confrontation was over, giving the impression that the Kaulikans had backed down. As he finished speaking, Eric moved to his side and said rather loudly, "Vani, everything is four-A-okay."

Griffin did not react to the comment. Rak completed his message to his unhappy Councillors and then the General walked them to the door.

"A last piece of advice," Griffin said. "Our union is vast but you have seen how we are a claustrophobic race. There are worlds everywhere, even in other galaxies. Find one far away."

Rak nodded. "*Then we will not meet again?*"

"I very much doubt it."

So Griffin really wasn't such a bad guy, after all, Eric thought. Eric couldn't resist. He slapped the General on the back and laughed. "Hell, you haven't seen the last of me."

Epilogue

Once they were back aboard the flagship, Rak excused himself. He had to speak to his fellow Councillors. Eric could well understand his haste. Eric would have enjoyed seeing their faces when they learned the truth. But Rak did not invite him to tag along and it appeared his part in these large matters was over. He was disappointed. In spite of the dozen nervous breakdowns he'd suffered during the last couple of days, he had enjoyed playing the big cheese.

A Kaulikan guard was waiting in the docking bay to escort him to his new quarters. Translator in hand, Eric asked to be taken to an observational window instead. He had not seen *Excalibur* on his return trip in the shuttle and it was clearly no longer in the flagship bay. As the old freighter had been so quickly removed into space, Vani might not have had a chance to reach Strem. The possibility was disquieting.

Before leaving for The Patrol battle cruiser, Eric had given Vani four slips of paper, each containing a different message. He had anticipated that after everything

191

was said and done, Griffin would try to keep him from his friends. The messages relayed four separate conclusions to the whole scenario: The Kaulikans got cheated and his new forwarding address was Mercury; the Kaulikans got cheated and now he was one of them; the Kaulikans got what they deserved and he was still heading for Mercury; the Kaulikans got what they deserved and he hoped Vani didn't get tired of him. He had placed the brightest possibility last because immediately after the vaporization of the factory, it had seemed the least likely. He had taught Vani the English words: One, two, three, four. When he had said four-A-okay in the General's quarters, she had known to deliver the last message to Strem *immediately*. The fourth message had also contained a note that Strem could respond to.

Eric's escort led him to a small dimly lit room whose one wall, from floor to ceiling, was a clear window looking out into space. Primitive telescopes that employed curved lenses to gather and magnify light were available for use. After assuring him that he would be waiting nearby, the guard left the room.

For the first time in a long time Eric found himself alone. Off to the far left of the window was the nova, still beautiful with its many hued halos, yet somehow less impressive to him. It was not logical, but he couldn't help feeling that he had defeated the volatile star. He remembered Rak's comment in the shuttle. The First Councillor had imagined that the sun had grown tired with its children's wicked ways, like an impatient parent. Well, Eric had never taken parental punishment easily and it gave him a deep satisfaction to have pulled a fast one on this Big Daddy. Even with their huge fleet, the Kaulikan race had stood only a slim chance of life. Now their survival was practically certain.

As to his own future . . . he had to know about those messages.

Turning toward darker regions Eric noted a faint cluster of silver slivers floating between the stars. He reached for a telescope and adjusted the focus, peering in the eyepiece. The Patrol Fleet had yet to activate their hyper drives. The reason was clear to the eye. A mercuric dot was leaving Griffin's command vessel for a dull gray stubby cylinder that floated nearby; no doubt a ferry being sent over to remove *Excalibur*'s crew. The General apparently did not trust his friends at the freighter's helm.

"So long, guys," he said, feeling a stab of loneliness. "We had a hell of a vacation."

A warm hand touched the side of his face. *"Eric."*

It was Vani, wearing an uncertain smile. They moved away from the window and sat on a nearby couch, the translator resting between them. Hopefully, the thing would keep working until he could learn the language.

"I spoke to Rak in the Council Chamber," Vani said, her eyes shining. *"He said that you have given us a new life."*

"Nice of him to give me all the credit."

She leaned forward, clasped his hands. *"When can we be at Lira?"*

"With the instructions you received, your people could probably outfit the flagship with the necessary drives in a few months. Of course, it will take longer to prepare every ship in the fleet, but once your engineers and technicians get the hang of the technology, it won't be long. You probably won't even end up at Lira. Somewhere else might be better, far away. Distance won't matter anymore."

Vani was happy, but her uncertainty remained. *"You say 'you' not 'we.' Are you not coming with us?"*

Eric took his hands back, folding them together on his lap, staring at the floor. He was afraid to ask about the notes. "I have no choice."

His answer distressd her. *"But is this not a choice you would make?"*

He felt ashamed of his self-centeredness. He turned to her. "Yes, it is. I love your people. I love . . . that I've been given the opportunity to stay here with you. But . . . I don't know."

"What?"

He laughed, once, embarrassed. "Vani, we met under unusual circumstances. Strem and I were stumbling around, lost. We intended to use you. We lied to you. Why, you didn't even know that I was an alien." Boy that sounded weird. "What I'm trying to say is that I like you, but I'm not one of you. I don't even have white hair."

"You have beautiful hair."

"My eyes are funny."

"You have beautiful eyes."

"Vani . . ."

"Eric." She took his hands again. *"I have watched you. Everything you did to help us you did because you thought we were a people as good as your people."*

"Right."

"Then why do you not think you are as good as we?"

She had a point there. "I guess I don't want you to feel you have to stay my friend now that the excitement is over." He added hastily, "If you don't want to, that is."

She laughed. *"You are my new job! When I spoke to Rak in the Council Chamber, he said it was my responsibility to help you adjust to our society."* She patted his arm. *"I would rather take care of you than take care of a fruit tree."*

He decided he would be a fool to argue with her further. "Vani," he said reluctantly, "I don't suppose you got a chance to give the notes to Strem?"

She laughed again, mimicking his code words in English, "Four-A-okay?"

"You got to him?"

She nodded, pulling a paper from her pants pocket. "Yes. And he returned the note to me after writing on the back."

Eric plucked the paper from her hand, unable to restrain himself. On the one side, in his own handwritings, was his message:

Strem,

If you get this note it means, no matter what you are told otherwise, the Kaulikans got the graviton and hyper drives, and that I have been exiled aboard their fleet. If this is now the case, I believe The Tachyon Web will eventually come down. Let's set up a rendezvous point, say the third planet from Lira—the Kaulikans' original destination. I'll be there every spring break, until we meet again.

Eric

P.S. —The above information must be kept secret.

He turned the paper over and read:

Eric,

They're getting ready to tow us out of here. Got to write fast. I'm glad you got Griffin to choke. What the hell, I guess there is plenty of room for everybody. If you got the goods on the drives, have the Kaulikans build you your own private starship.

Next spring break, or the one after that—whenever—sounds fine with me.

Strem

P.S. —Give Green Eyes a big juicy kiss for me.

Eric calmly folded the note and put it away. Then he burst out laughing. Strem's suggestion was in keeping with his own ideas. After all, Rak owed him one. Before the Kaulikans finished outfitting their fleet for supralight travel, they could whip up a small cruiser for him; nothing fancy, just something that could get him where he wanted to go, like, to the other side of the universe.

"*Good news?*" Vani asked.

"Vani, once you . . . once we get settled on our new world, how would a trip sound?"

"*Is this Strem's idea?*"

"Sort of."

She was interested. "*To where?*"

He looked out the window at the soft glowing body of The Milky Way. "I've always wanted to see the center of the galaxy."

She nodded. "*So have I.*"

"Great, that will be our first stop." He sat up with a start. The stars in the vicinity of The Patrol ships had begun to ripple and blur. Griffin was readying his cruisers for a hyper jump. Eric hurried to the telescope and was in time to catch a closeup view of the Earth Fleet, and *Excalibur*, as they bent space inside itself and blinked out of sight into another dimension. This time he experienced no stab of loneliness nor did he even feel the need to say good-bye once more. He would see his friends again. It was written in the stars.

"Did Strem say anything else?" Vani asked, leaning into his side. Eric put his arm around her. He owed it to Strem to fulfill his last request.

"As a matter of fact, he did."

ABOUT THE AUTHOR

CHRISTOPHER PIKE is the author of several novels for young adults, including *Chain Letter*, *Slumber Party*, and *Weekend*. *The Tachyon Web* is his first science fiction novel.

An Explosive Science Fiction Adventure

The ColSec Trilogy
by Douglas Hill

☐ *EXILES OF COLSEC* (25785-4 • $2.75)—They were outcasts from Earth, young rebels exiled against their will to a harsh and deadly planet filled with vicious aliens and monstrous creatures. To survive, they had to learn to trust one another, to join together. But their deadliest peril came from the world they'd left behind.

☐ *THE CAVES OF KLYDOR* (25929-6 • $2.75)—The rebels have found the key to survival. But in the danger-filled depths of the caves of Klydor, they found a mysterious stranger who would alter their destinies forever.

☐ *COLSEC REBELLION* (On sale November 15, 1986 • 26145-2 • $2.75)—The rebels have made Klydor their own. Now they have returned to the savage streets that spawned them to rally Earth's young to rebellion.

Buy all of the books in the *ColSec Trilogy*, on sale wherever Bantam Spectra Books are sold, or use the handy coupon below for ordering:

Bantam Books, Inc., Dept. SF4, 414 East Golf Road, Des Plaines, Ill. 60016

Please send me the books I have checked above. I am enclosing $_____ (please add $1.50 to cover postage and handling; send check or money order—no cash or C.O.D.'s please.)

Name _____

Address_____

City/State _____ Zip _____

SF4—11/86

Please allow four to six weeks for delivery. This offer expires 5/87. Prices and availability subject to change without notice.

The long-awaited new novel from
Hugo and Nebula Award-Winning Author

DAVID BRIN
THE POSTMAN

Here is the powerful story of a post-holocaust
United States, a shattered country slipping into a
new dark age—until one man, Gordon Krantz,
offers new hope for the future . . . using a symbol
from the vanished past.

THE POSTMAN—available November 1985 in
hardcover wherever Bantam Spectra Books are
sold.

Special Offer
Buy a Bantam Book
for only 50¢.

Now you can have Bantam's catalog filled with hundreds of titles plus take advantage of our unique and exciting bonus book offer. A special offer which gives you the opportunity to purchase a Bantam book for only 50¢. Here's how!

By ordering any five books at the regular price per order, you can also choose any other single book listed (up to a $4.95 value) for just 50¢. Some restrictions do apply, but for further details why not send for Bantam's catalog of titles today!

Just send us your name and address and we will send you a catalog!

BANTAM BOOKS, INC.
P.O. Box 1006, South Holland, Ill. 60473

Mr./Mrs./Miss/Ms. _____
(please print)

Address _____

City _____ State _____ Zip _____ FC(A)—11/88

Please allow four to six weeks for delivery.

THE UNFORGETTABLE FANTASY NOVELS OF
R. A. MacAvoy

☐ TEA WITH THE BLACK DRAGON (25403-0 • $2.95) "A refreshing change from the more familiar epic or heroic fantasy. I recommend it highly."—*San Francisco Chronicle*

☐ DAMIANO (25347-6 • $2.95) "A treasurable read. MacAvoy is undeniably a writer to watch for."—Anne McCaffrey

☐ DAMIANO'S LUTE (25977-6 • $2.95) "This is fantasy at its highest point."—Andre Norton

☐ RAPHAEL (25978-4 • $2.95) "This sequel to DAMIANO and DAMIANO'S LUTE concludes a remarkable trilogy full of warmth, gentle humor and MacAvoy's undeniable charm."—*Library Journal*

☐ DAMIANO BOXED SET (32332 • $8.45)

☐ THE BOOK OF KELLS (25260-7 • $3.50) "Strongly recommended to all. The strength of the novel lies in the credibility of both setting and character."—*Fantasy Review*

Buy these titles wherever Bantam Spectra Books are sold, or use the handy coupon below for ordering:

Bantam Books, Inc., Dept. SF8, 414 East Golf Road, Des Plaines, Ill. 60016

Please send me the books I have checked above. I am enclosing $_____ (Please add $1.50 to cover postage and handling). Send check or money order—no cash or C.O.D.'s please.

Mr/Ms _____

Address _____

City/State _____ Zip _____

SF8—10/86

Please allow four to six weeks for delivery. This offer expires 4/87. Prices and availability subject to change without notice.